"I hear you."

He pulled the keys to the front door from his pocket. "Will you be here tomorrow?"

"I'll be working."

"See you tomorrow, then. Sweet dreams."

Her green eyes sparkled in the light of the full moon filtering into her car. Her lips were full and ready to be kissed.

He stretched his arm out on the back of the seat. It would take one move to wrap it around Callie and pull her close to him. He wanted to kiss her, but his gut told him that his kiss wouldn't be welcome.

Not yet anyway.

Reed wasn't going to let Callie go this time. She filled the empty space that was ten years of his life. Sure, he loved to ride bulls, but something was missing.

And that was Callie Wainright.

Dear Reader,

I'd like to introduce you to Reed Beaumont, middle brother of the bull-riding Beaumont brothers. After being on the road since he was eighteen, riding with the Professional Bull Riders, will Reed settle down now at the age of twenty-eight?

But Reed has a deep-seated desire: he wants to beat his older brother's record in Vegas. This goal will take him away from Callie Wainright in approximately two months.

Callie was Reed's first love, and the same goes for Callie. Reed asked her to join him on the road after high school, but she needed roots—something she's never had during her twenty-eight years.

Will these two ever get together? Will a long-distance relationship work?

These are all problems that Callie and Reed have to figure out—or should they go their separate ways?

I love to hear from readers! Contact me at chris@christinewenger.com or at PO Box 1823, Cicero, New York.

Cowboy up!

Chris Wenger

REUNITED WITH THE BULL RIDER

—

CHRISTINE WENGER

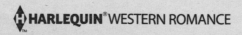

HARLEQUIN® WESTERN ROMANCE

Recycling programs
for this product may
not exist in your area.

ISBN-13: 978-1-335-69964-0

Reunited with the Bull Rider

Copyright © 2018 by Christine Wenger

Printed in U.S.A.

Christine Wenger has worked in the criminal justice field for more years than she cares to remember, but now spends her time reading, writing and seeing the sights in our beautiful world. A native Central New Yorker, she loves watching professional bull riding and rodeo with her favorite cowboy, her husband, Jim. You can reach Chris at PO Box 1823, Cicero, NY 13039, or through her website at christinewenger.com.

Books by Christine Wenger

Harlequin Western Romance

Gold Buckle Cowboys
The Cowboy and the Cop

Harlequin Special Edition

Gold Buckle Cowboys
The Rancher's Surprise Son
Lassoed into Marriage
How to Lasso a Cowboy
The Cowboy Code

The Hawkins Legacy
The Tycoon's Perfect Match
It's That Time of Year
Not Your Average Cowboy
The Cowboy and the CEO
The Cowboy Way

Visit the Author Profile page
at Harlequin.com for more titles.

To all cowboys and cops,

Be careful out there!

And to Michele Goldstein, new friend,
who keeps smiling through every challenge.
Chocolate will help!

Chapter One

"Callie Wainright, what the hell are you doing in my home?"

Callie jumped at the low and lethal voice. She spun around and found herself toe-to-toe with Reed Beaumont.

Reed. Seeing him so unexpectedly, so near, she couldn't swallow. They'd gone to school together since they were first graders in Beaumont, Oklahoma, up until the summer after senior year of high school when things got too serious too fast. Then they'd parted ways.

Callie had thought she could handle seeing Reed again if they ever met face-to-face for any length of time, but she couldn't find her voice.

He was the middle brother of the bull-riding Beaumonts. The Professional Bull Riders' announcers called them the Beaumont Big Guns, and they were breaking records with every ride.

Big brother Luke was solid and responsible and a recent bridegroom. Younger brother Jesse was footloose with a devil-may-care attitude. Reed was a healthy mix of the two. There wasn't a soul in the town that was named after their founding ancestor, Ezra Beaumont, who didn't follow their careers, including Callie.

"R-Reed." She swallowed hard. "Reed. Hello. It's been a long time."

She looked into his eyes for several beats of her heart. She remembered them as mostly calm and comforting, but the blue pools were turbulent, just like that sunny day that had changed the direction of both their lives.

Callie's normally poised and businesslike manner was nowhere to be found, and she was afraid that her suddenly weak knees would give out.

"Why you are in my father's study and sitting in his chair? What are you doing at the Beaumont Ranch?" His voice was cold and icy; obviously he'd never forgiven her. In spite of all their wonderful plans for the future, Callie had backed out at the last minute. She'd stayed home to take care of her mother and gone to community college. She had been supposed to go on the road with him, but she hadn't able to.

Not when her family had needed her—and they still needed her.

She'd had obligations in Beaumont back then. She still had the same obligations, only now she had a mortgage and she was working hard to pay for it.

"In answer to your question, I'm working here for a while."

Recently, Luke had hired her for the job of her dreams. When he was in town last year, restoring the ranch after Hurricane Daphne, he'd heard of her work as an executive helper, along with her top-notch business, Personable Assistance.

Yes. She was now sitting in Big Dan Beaumont's office on an overstuffed brown leather executive chair on the historic Beaumont Ranch. Several patriarchs had sat behind the great oak Stickley desk.

The ranch was the pride of little Beaumont. As a tourist

attraction, it brought much-needed dollars to various shops, restaurants and cafés in the area.

The Beaumonts needed her and she needed them. When word got around town that she'd been hired at the ranch, Callie's Personable Assistance would skyrocket. Maybe she'd even have to hire some help.

She pointed to the crutches he was leaning on. "Bull-riding accident, Reed?" she asked to fill the silence.

"Yeah. But how about elaborating on my question—what are you doing here?"

"I'm a personal assistant. I was hired to get everything organized," she said. "And to digitize the ranch's records."

When Luke had shown her what he'd wanted her to do, Callie had noticed that the Beaumonts' record keeping was an outright train wreck. All income and expenditures needed to be organized and entered on a spreadsheet.

She was good at that.

Callie gestured to the pile of mail sliding from the desk to the floor like an avalanche. There were opened and unopened sympathy cards and mass cards in memory of Valerie Lynn Beaumont, Big Dan's wife. Valerie Lynn had died over three years ago.

"I'll send thank-you cards to what needs to be answered," she told Luke. "Like the mass cards or monetary gifts."

There was more mail in the three feed sacks leaning on the right wall. Luke had pulled them out of his pickup, hoisted all three on his shoulder and deposited them, explaining that it was fan mail from the Professional Bull Riders' office for Reed, Jesse and himself.

Callie remembered telling Luke, "I'll answer all the fan mail with an autographed picture of whomever the mail is addressed to. And then there's email that comes via your outdated websites. I'll answer that, too, and get your them into this century."

Reed cleared his throat. "Who hired you?"

"Your brother Luke."

"But Luke's on his honeymoon," he said coolly.

"I know. He hired me before he left for Hawaii with Amber. I think that it was Amber—or should I call her Sheriff Beaumont?—who suggested me." She stood and rubbed her forehead. "What's the problem, Reed? Do you think I broke into this office because I was just dying to answer fan mail for you and your brothers?"

"Guess not." Reed aimed his crutches in the direction of a brown leather wingback chair and flopped down with a grunt. He stretched out his right leg.

"So, Callie. Tell me. What have you been doing these past ten years?"

CALLIE LOOKED AS beautiful as always, Reed thought. His fingers itched to bury his fingers in her mass of blond curls like he'd done before. Her eyes had always reminded him of the spring-green grass along the Beaumont River on the eastern side of the ranch.

Today, Callie had on a pair of jeans that she'd been born to wear, jeans that enhanced her curves. He liked her long-sleeved shirt; the pink-and-blue plaid looked soft enough to touch. And she wore cowboy boots. Callie always wore boots. She said that it made her look taller than her five-foot-five-inch frame.

"I've been living my life, Reed. Going to school and working."

"You look great." And she did. But even more than looks, Callie was a good person inside and out. He'd developed a deep respect for her back when they were in grammar school together, and finally found the nerve to ask her out on a "real" date in senior year. What had followed was three months of romance and a summer full of heat that they generated themselves.

Callie had been his first, and he was hers.

He'd liked the fact that she always volunteered to help someone in need, but she would never ask for anything for herself. He'd missed her, missed their long walks and longer talks. He should have called her, but he couldn't, not after the way they'd parted.

"Thanks. You look great, too." She glanced at his injured leg. "Well, except for the obvious." She sighed. "I always tune into the PBR, but I must have missed the news about your leg."

"It's my knee. Torn meniscus. I might not need surgery if I take it easy on the leg and keep it up."

"Let me get you another chair so you can stretch out."

Before he could tell her not to bother, she pulled over the other seat.

With a groan, he put his leg up and tried to get comfortable. "Thanks, but you never answered my question. How've you been?"

"I've been…fine. But I really should get back to work. And to clarify things, Luke hired me to clean up all the papers in here and get them all organized."

Callie didn't say much, but he knew she had a habit of changing the subject when she didn't want to answer a question. Like now.

"Good. This place needs organizing. There are still… things…from my mother's…um, death, like cards and all. We just couldn't bring ourselves to go through everything, least of all my father. After Hurricane Daphne hit, we just dried out whatever papers looked important and tossed the rest."

Silence.

Callie cleared her throat. "Big Dan is still in rehab, isn't he?"

She asked that question probably to break the silence this time. She had that habit, too. She knew the answer already. Beaumont was a small town. But Callie cared about people, so her question was genuine. All his feelings for her came rushing back like a tidal wave. Was she dating someone? Was she glad to see him? "Yeah. Alcohol rehab. My father's been there for seven months, but it seems like he's been fighting his demons forever." Truthfully, he was worried about his dad. He'd had several setbacks, but they'd be worth it if he learned something from them. Reed wasn't sure that his dad realized that he could actually get a sentence of incarceration if he was found guilty of violating his probation.

"I understand about Big Dan. And you know, Reed, I can't believe I'm here, either. I came to the ranch on the usual visits we had every two years in school during history class. Your beautiful mother gave us the tour. I've always loved the ranch."

A pang of sorrow hit his heart, as it always did whenever he thought of his mother, and he took a deep breath. "Mom loved to share the Beaumont history. And remember how I had to take the tour, too? Sometimes I gave it!"

She laughed.

"Callie, I'm sorry I reacted so weirdly. I just didn't expect to see you, but I'm glad I did. So you've been okay?"

"I've been fine." She nodded.

"According to the town grapevine, I know you've never gotten married, but are you dating anyone these days? Weren't you engaged once?"

His mom had seen Callie's engagement announcement in the *Beaumont Bulletin*, and Mom had called him—a couple of times—to tell him. Immediately, he fell into a riding slump, drank way too much beer and had to climb out of his funk with the help of his riding pals and his brothers.

"I'm between serious relationships." She laughed, but her eyes suddenly misted. "It's a long, boring story."

"I have the time."

She shook her head. "I don't. I have work to do."

It was like pulling teeth with a bull rope, trying to get her to expand on her replies, but he'd find out sooner or later. On occasion, Reed had seen Callie in town. They would wave to each other, but they'd never stopped to talk. She'd always seemed like she was in a hurry to get away from him.

There wasn't anything more to say to each other after their disastrous split. He'd been hurt to his very soul when she'd stayed in Beaumont. Or maybe he'd been just too damn young and idealistic to think that she'd travel with him, that'd he'd win a lot of money and they'd start a family.

He'd achieved two out of those three.

"Callie, did you ever go to college for advertising and marketing, like you wanted?"

"No. I didn't. I went to Beaumont Community College and took some business classes."

"Why not advertising and marketing?"

She shrugged and looked away, not meeting his eyes. "Things happened," she said quietly. "And BCC didn't offer advertising and marketing."

"But you dreamed of working at an ad agency on Madison Avenue someday."

"It doesn't matter anymore," she said softly. "I have my own business now."

"Good for you. Callie. You always managed to land on your feet."

"Most of the time."

Reed could see how uncomfortable he'd made her, so it was his turn to change the subject. "So whose personal assistant are you exactly?"

"Luke's. He was the one who hired me, although I seem to be doing things for your family." She pointed to the three overstuffed feed bags. "Those are full of fan mail. The Beaumont Big Guns are quite the hit."

"That's all…ours?"

"Yes. And it's loaded with SASEs for autographed pictures and your reply."

"Huh?"

"Self-addressed stamped envelopes."

"Oh."

"I understand there's even more mail at the PBR office. They're shipping it here."

"Wow! I am totally shocked."

"You shouldn't be. It seems like the whole country is cheering for you three."

"Tell me, what else does a personal assistant do?" Reed asked with a wink and a grin.

"Not *that*!" He liked getting a rise out of her. He wasn't disappointed. Callie's cell phone rang. "Excuse me.

"Hello? Yes. Hi, Luke…He's here right now…Yes… He's supposed to keep his leg up?…Oh?…I'll tell him… Luke, should he do that considering his injury?…Okay, yeah, I'll get him there…But I wasn't hired to be Reed's… nanny." She clicked off her phone and turned to Reed.

"Do you have your cell phone on?"

"I can't find it."

"Apparently your agent, Rick…um…"

"Kessler."

She nodded. "Mr. Kessler has been trying to call you.

He phoned Luke in the hope that Luke could get hold of you. Mr. Kessler wanted to remind you that today you're supposed to go to the local public TV station and be interviewed."

"Dammit! I forgot about that!"

She checked her watch. "You have to be there in an hour. You might want to—"

"Shower and shave?" he asked.

"Might be a good idea since you are going to be on television."

"I remember now." He adjusted his crutches to get up from the chair. "They are doing a segment on bull riding."

"Here's some more news, Reed. I am now *your* personal assistant, too. In addition to my other duties here in your father's office, I am supposed to 'facilitate your recovery,' according to your agent and Luke." There was an incredulous tone to her voice, like she couldn't believe she had to add Reed's circumstances to her original duties. "Also, Mr. Kessler is worried that you keep missing your appointments and public appearances. And you are supposed to keep your leg elevated. I also have to make sure you make the appearances that your agent arranged. Sounds like a contradiction. And I'll be getting paid extra."

"Then I'll make it worth your while!"

"Don't even think about it," she said. "But tell me about your knee."

"The medical staff think that my meniscus might heal on its own. I'll need surgery if it doesn't."

"Then you'll have to keep it up whenever possible. Now, go and take a shower, and make it quick. And if it sounds like I'm nagging you, it's because I am!"

Reed saluted her. "Yes, ma'am."

He hated being laid up, but he was getting a kick out of the fact that she agreed to look out for him. "I'm getting back to the PBR as soon as I can. The Beaumont brothers have the first three slots tied up. I can't stay on the injured list for any length of time or some young rider will take my place."

"I hear you, but first things first. I'll get you to the TV station, since you can't drive with a torn meniscus."

"Yes, ma'am." He tweaked his hat with his thumb and forefinger, and crutched to his room, where he'd tossed his duffel bag.

After pulling out clean clothes, he went to the bathroom off the bedroom he would forever think of as his. He shucked off his clothes and adjusted the shower water until it was just lukewarm.

No matter how far away he was, he always wanted a home to come back to, and the Beaumont Ranch was the place. For some reason, it felt even more like home with Callie here.

And if it wasn't for Amber, they would have lost the ranch completely in a tax auction. Thankfully, Amber had made it a point to go to a PBR event and told Luke that he'd better get back and rescue the ranch, not only from the auction block but from the damage that Hurricane Daphne had done eighteen months prior.

Luke had contacted Jesse and Reed, and the "Three Musketeers" sprang into action and sank every penny they received from their bull-riding winnings into fixing up the ranch.

Reed took the fastest shower of his life. He got dressed, grabbed his crutches and went back to Big Dan's study, where he found Callie hard at work.

CALLIE'S HEART DID a little leap in her chest when she looked up and saw Reed in the study.

His hair was sticking up in places and it was still wet. He looked…gorgeous.

He wore a long-sleeved baby blue shirt that stretched across his muscled chest.

"So, you're my new personal assistant?" He grinned, then winked.

"Don't go all juvenile on me."

"But we'll have fun," Reed said.

"Don't bug me, Reed."

"Is that a challenge?" he asked.

"It's a fact."

"We'll see about that, Miss Callie. We'll see."

Callie couldn't help peeking as Reed walked to the front door. That cowboy could really work a pair of jeans, even on crutches. No wonder the buckle bunnies were always after him. Reed was one hunk of a man.

But she wasn't interested. Her past love life was like a soap opera and she was canceling the show. She didn't want to think about her past relationships now, if ever.

Callie found her car keys in the deep recesses of her purse and held the door open so Reed could crutch through. His aftershave wafted around her. Pine and leather. Strong scents. Strong, like Reed.

No. She wasn't going to think things like that. He was just a client, not boyfriend material. He hadn't been after high school and nothing had changed. In fact, she was even more wary of getting involved with yet another man.

Callie was just tired of putting effort into another relationship. She was tired, just plain tired.

Reed's magnetism was lethal and, therefore, Callie

had to be extra cautious. She had to reinforce that wall around her and wear a Kevlar vest to protect her heart.

They both slid into her ancient SUV and Callie turned the key. It started with a moan and a groan, but it started. She patted the dashboard. "Good job, Ruby."

"Ruby?" Reed asked as she aimed the vehicle toward the long exit out of the ranch.

"It used to be red, but now it's mostly faded to pink. I should call it Pinky."

He grinned. "I'm guessing that it's about ten years old."

"Close. It's twelve years old."

He chuckled. "You really should put it out of its misery."

"Then what do I drive?" she asked.

"Another car. Maybe something newer."

"When you find a money tree, let me know where it is."

"Oh, I see. Sorry." Reed was quiet for quite a while before he started talking again.

"Callie, I'll never forget the day and night of our senior prom. I loved taking you and showing you off. And at graduation, when you were valedictorian, your speech was a pitch for the graduates to stay in Beaumont and make it bigger and better. I liked that."

"I figure that only about one-third of them moved. I've kept track throughout the years. Some even returned."

Reed snapped his fingers. "Let's throw a reunion. We can have it at the practice arena on the ranch. I'll order some tents. It'd be great to see everyone."

"You want to have a party on the same spot where you practice riding bulls?"

"Yeah. I don't have any practice bulls here yet, if it's the manure you're thinking of."

Callie couldn't plan a party right now. She had enough work to do being the personal assistant to the Beaumonts. "Um, uh…maybe when I have everything organized, having a reunion is something to think about."

"Don't you ever have fun, Callie?"

"Basically…no. Not since high school. I've been juggling many balls in the air. I have responsibilities and obligations."

"Responsibilities and obligations? Sounds serious."

"It is. They are." She decided to change the subject because she sounded like such a dud. Maybe she was, but such was life. "I liked the prom. If I remember correctly, Tiffany McGrath, head cheerleader, was the prom queen and you were king."

"I wonder what Tiff is doing now."

"She lives on Maple Street and has three kids. She married Josh Nelson. Remember how everyone called him Nerdy Nelson? He's not. He's a full-time investment broker and a volunteer firefighter. Tiff has her own gift shop on Main Street— Gifts by Tiff."

"Tiff had dreams of working for the United Nations. She was studying three languages." He shook his head. "She wanted to move out of Beaumont and go to a big city."

"Things change, Reed. People change. She told me that she wanted to raise her family in Beaumont."

"That's nice." He paused, as if he were thinking, then asked, "Do you ever regret not going to New York?"

"Maybe, but here I have responsibilities and—"

"Obligations," Reed finished.

"Yes."

She couldn't leave if she wanted to. She was entrenched in Beaumont, and her mother had her own local doctors who'd saved her from breast cancer ten years ago, and she hoped they'd be able to do it again now.

Her twin brothers would be leaving for college soon, but Beaumont was where they loved to be right now—in the small bungalow on Elm that she'd bought for them. Well, the bank owned it, but as long as she kept working as hard as she had been and kept up with the taxes and the monthly payments, no one would ever evict them again.

Never.

"Is the TV station still on Wells Avenue?" Reed asked.

"Yes. And we're cutting the time short. You won't have much time to prepare."

"I've done a million of these things. I don't need to prepare. 'Reed, what made you become a bull rider?' I'll answer, 'I love the adrenaline rush and the friends that I've made. And being with my brothers is another reason why I love riding. To love what you're doing and make money doing it…well, it doesn't get any better than that.'"

Callie chuckled. "I guess you don't need to prepare after all."

"If he asks me that question first, I'll buy us coffee."

"If he asks you that first, I'll buy us lunch," Callie said in a moment of exuberance she hadn't felt in a long time. Goofy bets with Reed had been some of the best times of her teen years, and no one else she'd dated since he'd left had made her laugh like he had.

Callie parked in front of the station and they both hurried into the lobby, where Reed was whisked away to the booth. Callie was directed to a viewing room, where she settled into a comfy chair.

The announcer nodded to Reed. "With us is champion bull rider Reed Beaumont. Reed, tell the audience why you decided to ride bulls."

Reed looked at Callie through the window of the

booth, grinned and winked. Then he launched into his memorized speech.

Callie enjoyed watching him. He was in his element, casual and charming, informative and humble. She could tell he was excited about all aspects of bull riding and appreciated the PBR.

She used to be that excited about studying advertising and marketing. The internet had made everything so exciting. Besides, facts and figures were her strong suit, and developing spreadsheets was exhilarating. And who didn't adore pie charts?

She studied Reed. He was sitting on a chair with wheels and his left arm was up in the air. Callie could hear how he was retelling one of his rides on Cowabunga, his nemesis.

Reed's face was animated; his now sapphire eyes were twinkling—it was clear he simply loved the sport.

Then his interview was over and he stared at his crutches for a few seconds before he picked them up. She was probably the only one who noticed the slump of his shoulders and the droop at the corners of his mouth when he looked at them.

He wanted to be riding bulls. Even Beaumont probably ran second place to his love of riding bulls.

"Callie, do you want to grab that lunch you owe me? I'm famished. It's on me because you drove me here."

"It's on me. I lost the bet. Besides, I don't need any payback."

"I know, but I'd like to treat you."

She smiled. "I really should get back to work."

"You pick the place," Reed said as if he hadn't heard her.

"If you like Italian food, I'd suggest Poppa Al's Restaurant on Main and Willow."

"Sounds great." He moved, but his crutches didn't. She could see the pain register on his face and how it hurt when his right leg bore some weight.

They walked toward Callie's SUV. "I'm hoping that this thing heals fast because I keep my rank." He stopped walking and turned to her. "Okay, who's your favorite rider?"

"Probably your brother Luke," she lied. "He can ride anything with hair."

Reed put his hands over his heart. "I'm wounded."

"Yes, you are." She pointed to his leg, then aimed the key fob at her ancient SUV to unlock it. Sometimes it worked; sometimes it didn't. Today it didn't, so she unlocked the driver's side manually and leaned over to open the passenger side for Reed.

"You need to let your knee heal. You shouldn't have done that interview."

Reed sighed. "Rick said it'd be good publicity for us and for the PBR. I was committed to it."

"Committed to it? You didn't even remember—"

"That's why I need a personal assistant, Callie. I got so much on my mind."

"By going back to riding too soon, wouldn't you be jeopardizing your life? I mean, if you have a knee injury that hasn't healed yet, when your ride is over, can you hurry and run away before the bull pounds you into the dirt?" Callie asked.

"I might be a little slow getting away."

"Then you are jeopardizing the lives of the bullfighters whose job it is to protect you."

He paused for a while. "I'll give them a heads-up. But you have to remember that almost every bull rider rides with injuries."

"I suppose so, Reed, but I hate to see you hurt."

"It almost sounds like you care."

"Yeah, I care. I do. I don't want to see *any* of you riders hurt."

Reed put his hand on her shoulder and left it there for several beats. Her mouth suddenly went dry and her heart pounded in her ears.

She steeled herself and sternly reminded her heart that she'd had four serious relationships that never ended at the altar for various reasons.

And she was counting Reed, too. He'd been the first one.

Callie didn't want Reed touching her, even if it was on top of a blouse and a sleeveless plaid vest. She'd sworn off men.

She was going to ignore him as best as she could while working in his house. She had to clean up Big Dan's study and, by doing so, referrals to her business would soar.

She could pay her mortgage, maybe pay it off sooner that she needed to. Maybe she could even buy a bigger house.

And she could pay medical bills, her mother's medical bills from her recent cancer treatments and her brothers' from their sports injuries.

It seemed like a good plan. She'd just have to stay away from Reed and all the distractions that came with him.

Easy, right?

Chapter Two

Reed wondered why Callie seemed so nervous.

When he'd put his hand on her shoulder, he'd thought she was going to jump as high as Cowabunga.

He'd just felt as if he'd known her forever, which was true. He remembered her shyness that first day of school at the huge building his ancestor Charlie Beaumont had erected for grades kindergarten through twelve. Everyone growing up in Beaumont went to that brick monstrosity on the hill. The next nearest school was in Waterville, a three-hour drive away.

That first day, Callie had clung to the wall like a coat of paint. Reed had taken her hand and led her to a seat because, as a member of the First Family of Beaumont, that's what he did.

Reed wondered if Callie remembered that.

They'd kept a friendship brewing until a month before high school ended. They'd been inseparable that short summer until he'd left for the PBR.

He'd gone on the circuit; she'd stayed.

Could they pick up where they'd left off?

That was unrealistic. That bull had left the chute.

Callie never talked much about her problems. However, gossip had swirled when the story about her father taking up with a rich, older woman, Tish Holcomb, and leaving his family with a lot of credit card debt got around town.

In contrast, Reed's life was an open book. He was usually in the spotlight due to his world ranking with the PBR. To him, there wasn't a question that was off-limits, other than the name of who he was dating.

There were always a lot of women hanging around him whenever he went out or whenever he was autographing. Truth be told, he'd rarely dated. He was too busy keeping his rank. Every minute of his life was devoted to becoming a better bull rider.

He loved traveling with his brothers on the circuit— they had a lot of laughs and traded riding tips—but he definitely wanted to win the PBR Finals. To expedite his goal, he jogged. He worked out. He rode practice bulls, and while other riders, including his little brother, Jesse, were partying, Reed was doing yoga and pushups in his hotel room.

If he'd partied like Jesse, he couldn't ride the next morning. Maybe it was because Jesse was two years younger.

It was Reed's turn to win the Finals. He wanted to get out from under Luke's shadow. Maybe he'd catch a break and Luke wouldn't return to the PBR after his honeymoon.

No. He'd rather beat him fair and square.

Luke was riding high. He'd married the woman of his dreams, Beaumont Sheriff's Deputy Amber Chapman just after the World Finals in Vegas last November. With seven months of marriage under his belt, Luke was riding high with Amber.

Reed constantly wondered when it would be his turn to fall in love with a special person, like Luke had. No matter how much he loved riding bulls, he'd give it all up in a heartbeat to start a family.

He longed to model his kids' childhoods with the one he'd had. He and his brothers had had the whole Beaumont Ranch as their playground. They'd ridden horses, bikes, ATVs and various ranch equipment. The cowboys who worked the ranch had told them stories about the "golden days" of the Beaumont Ranch.

Those had been the carefree days…before his mother had died.

When Valerie Lynn was kicked in the head by a horse over three years ago and died, his family had never been the same. His father, Big Dan, had developed an alcohol problem and was now a ghost of his former robust self.

Big Dan hadn't wanted the ranch repaired and fixed to the way it had been. He'd wanted it left the same as the second his beloved wife died. It had been left the same, until Hurricane Daphne hit soon after. Then Big Dan was about to lose the ranch to taxes.

That was when the Three Musketeers had stepped in, pooled their money and become the owners of the ranch.

He marveled at the comfortable silence between Callie and him. Any other woman would find it necessary to fill the quiet with mindless chatter.

Reed was simply content to ride through Beaumont with Callie, seeing old haunts and marveling at new construction—new to him at least.

His stomach growled and Callie laughed. "I think you'll like Poppa Al's Restaurant, Reed. Their specialty is chicken parm. It's delicious."

"Chicken parm sounds good to me," he said.

They both got out of the car and, as he retrieved his crutches, he cursed the famed Cowabunga under his breath for his damaged knee.

"What's the matter?" Callie asked. "You doing okay?"

"I'm sick of these crutches already. I could go without them, but it hurts like the devil. Hell, it hurts like the devil *with* them."

"Then use the crutches, Reed." Callie jogged a few steps ahead and opened the door to make it easier to pass through.

He walked through. "Thanks."

"No problem."

A man came out from behind the bar, took Reed's hand and began pumping it. "Well, if it isn't Reed Beaumont, the great bull rider! It's about time you visited my place."

It took a split second for Reed to recognize Alphonse Giacomo. They'd played football together on the high school team. According to the *Beaumont Bulletin*, which he read online to keep current with the happenings of his hometown when he was on the road, Al had gone on to play professionally, but an injury had forced him to retire.

"And Callie Wainright!" He pulled Callie into a big bear hug. "It's good to see you again. My Susan was just talking about hiring you to keep our books straight. She doesn't trust me to do it correctly and thinks we're going to land in federal prison. That's my wife, five feet three inches and one hundred twenty-five pounds of total worry."

They all laughed.

"Have her call me." A business card appeared in Callie's hand and she held it out to Al. He took it and slipped into the pocket of his checked pants.

"We'll call you for sure, Callie."

"So, you're Poppa Al?" Reed asked, adjusting his crutches.

"Guilty as charged. I only wanted to open a spumoni

stand, but look at this!" He spread his arms wide to show how big his place was. "I can hold two wedding receptions at the same time—or one huge one."

Al looked from Callie to Reed and back again. His thick black eyebrows rose as he rubbed his hands together in glee. "So, are you here to book your wedding?"

"Uh…um…" Callie began, a blush starting on her neck then settling on her cheeks. "No."

Reed just laughed. "We're here for your chicken parm."

"You'll love it," Al said. "I make it from scratch. And I'll make you an antipasto to share. It's on the house. Now sit. Sit in the first booth. It's very romantic."

Al disappeared through swinging metal doors and Reed turned to Callie. "Shall we sit in the romantic booth?"

Callie shrugged. "Al seems to have made up his mind that we're to sit there."

Unlike Reed, Callie didn't seem to be enjoying Al's funny misunderstanding.

Reed winked. "Then let's not disappoint him," he said as he hung his crutches from the coat hook.

They both slid into the red vinyl booth with the white Formica table. "I hope we don't get indigestion from the romantic booth," he added, grinning.

"It'd be a shame if we did. It would spoil the experience." Callie's eyes twinkled.

Reed enjoyed her lighter mood.

He looked around and was impressed. "I didn't know Al Giacomo owned this place."

"Al just opened a couple months ago. In another hour, there'll be a line around the building. The word is out that if you want a good meal in Beaumont, go to Al's."

"This is a nice surprise, Callie. I'd lost touch with Al.

Actually, I've lost touch with many of my pals in Beaumont. Too much traveling, another circle of friends and I don't get home all that much."

"How long are you going to be here this time?"

"Probably three months. I'm planning on going back after the summer break. Since I'm healing, I figure it's my turn to work on the ranch. Luke did the majority of fixing up the ranch house after Hurricane Daphne, along with the barn. I am going to do more work on the barn and supervise fixing up the ramrod's house. Luke said it needs a new roof and some remodeling inside. Then Jesse will take his turn and work on an addition to our bull breeding facility, and a new bunkhouse for the hired hands. The old one's coming down."

"You're just about rebuilding the whole ranch."

A waitress came and dropped off frosty classes of water. "Hi, Callie."

"How are you doing, Darlene?" Callie said then turned to Reed. "Dar's grandparents retired here and Dar is living with them for the summer. She's working and going to Oklahoma State in the fall."

"Nice. What are you taking up?" Reed asked.

Her cheeks turned pink. "Um, uh…in hospital…hospitality, I mean. Hospitality."

Reed made eye contact with Callie, whose hands were over her mouth. She knew Darlene was having a hard time being a cool fan, whereas Reed was used to different reactions.

Some fans were terribly nervous; others were blatantly sexually aggressive. Luckily, more were nervous. He could deal with those fans, but the young ones who came on to him? Well, those made *him* nervous.

Darlene turned to Reed and giggled. "Uh… I've never done this before, but could I have your autograph, Reed?"

"Sure!"

"Wait here. Don't move!" she ordered.

Callie burst out laughing then sobered. "We're eating here, so we're not going to move. Did she forget that? I wonder if it's your celebrity or your handsomeness that has Darlene so overwhelmed."

"It's both. I'm sure it's both," Reed deadpanned, then raised an eyebrow. "But you think I'm handsome?"

"I…um…uh…"

Darlene returned out of breath and saved Callie from more stammering. She handed Reed a white foam take-out box.

"A take-out box?" Callie grinned. "But, Darlene, we haven't had our meal yet."

"I know, but this is all I could find for Reed to sign." She handed him the box and a ballpoint pen. "J-just don't press too h-hard or you'll p-punch a hole in the top."

He wrote his usual "Thanks for being a fan! Best wishes, Reed Beaumont" then added the city and date. He also added her name.

Smiling and holding out his hand, he waited several seconds before she realized what to do. She wiped her hands on her black apron and then held one out to him. They shook as she grinned widely.

"I am sorry to bother you again, but can I take a picture of you?"

"Absolutely."

She positioned her cell phone and pushed the icon several times. "Thanks, uh… Reed."

"But don't you want to be in the picture, too, Darlene?" Reed asked.

"Can I?"

"C'mon."

Without a word Darlene handed her cell phone to Callie.

Callie stifled another grin. "Sure, I'd be glad to take your picture with Reed.

Callie took four pictures of Reed sitting in the booth with Darlene next to him, then handed back the phone.

"Thanks, Reed."

"You're welcome, Darlene."

Darlene scurried away, her cell phone next to her heart.

Every once in a while, Callie realized what a celebrity Reed was. Not only did he receive bags full of fan mail, but obviously women fawned over him. Everyone knew that he was a real athlete in a very dangerous sport, but to Callie, he was Reed Beaumont, the man who chose riding bulls over her. Reed sat back in the booth. "Sorry about that."

"Sorry…about what? Oh, you mean about Darlene? You were very sweet to her. She'll remember this moment for a lifetime."

"I hope not."

"I was her age once. I know."

"Now, what were we talking about? Oh, yes. The PBR and you, I think," she said.

"Since I had the summer off from the PBR, I wanted to catch a couple rides on some of the other circuits so I could boost my points, but my injury put a halt to those plans."

Callie nodded. "If you do what you're supposed to, you'll be healthy for the PBR when things start back up. It's only the end of May. You can do it if you'd stay off of it and rest."

"Will you hold my hand if I have to go to the hospital?"

"Oh! The brave, big-shot bull rider is too chicken to have surgery!"

"No," he said quickly, softly. "I'm just too chicken to go to the same hospital where my mother died."

Callie met his eyes. "I'm sorry, Reed. I didn't think."

He put his hand over hers. "I'm sorry, too. I didn't mean to blurt that out. *I* was the one who didn't think."

She put her hand over his. "Obviously it's bothering you. You could go to another hospital."

"And not go to the one that Great-Gramps Cyrus Beaumont built? I'd be drummed out of the family, or what's left of it."

SHE REMOVED HER hand when the antipasto came and he felt deprived of her warmth. He knew she was only embarrassed for what she'd said, but he liked the feel of hers over his.

He looked down at the large platter. A mountain of lettuce was heaped high, a display of various meats, cheeses, tomatoes, tuna and veggies artfully piled on top.

Reed sighed. "Does Al expect us to eat all this plus a meal?"

"Yes. He does." Callie picked up the big fork and spoon on the side of the platter.

"No wonder it's the romantic booth. We could live here in this booth for a week eating one meal."

"You on one side on the booth and me on the other?" Callie giggled. "That's not very romantic! We should be on the same side at least, just like the front seat of a car."

"I remember many great times with you in the front seat of my car!"

She laughed.

Reed thought Callie's playful spirit was slowly returning and that made him glad. She seemed so sad sometimes, and guilt would overwhelm him as he was responsible for some of that.

He remembered how Callie was always hell bent on helping others and working hard, and he loved that about her, to a point. He didn't want her to overextend herself and make herself sick. On top of that, he knew how much she anguished about her mother's health, worried about her brothers and paying for their injuries, and was anxious about keeping a roof over all their heads. Nothing ever changed with her.

But all that angst was part of Callie, but so was the laughter and joy, and the latter was what he wanted to bring out. He wanted to make her smile and laugh and forget about her worries for a while.

The chicken parm came on two more platters, one for Callie and one for Reed. A mountain of spaghetti was stacked on the side.

"It's amazing that you, Jesse and Luke are the first three in the standings. What are the odds of that?" Callie asked twirling some spaghetti with her fork.

Reed tried the chicken. Delicious. "I don't have a clue about the odds, but I like the fact that the Beaumont Big Guns are in the top three. And Luke was even going to retire after he got married, but I'm guessing that he's going to give the Finals another go. So, he's riding in another circuit to keep in the game while on an extended honeymoon. Amber is traveling with him and they are having a great time. She loves it."

Callie sat as still as a statue.

"We could have had a great time, too, Callie."

She shook her head. "My father left us with thousands of dollars in credit card debt from his gambling addiction before he split for Tahiti with Tish Holcomb, rich widow and my father's latest meal ticket. Besides, Reed, admit it—we were too young."

"We might have been young, but we were certainly mature." He sighed. "Your father should have paid his own debts, not saddle you and your mother with them."

"I agree, but most of the cards were in my mother's name, and the creditors were tormenting us."

He sighed. "You could have followed me at any time. We talked about that, but I didn't hear from you and I missed you."

"The phone works both ways, Reed. You could have called me, but the Beaumont grapevine said that you had the company of your buckle bunnies."

"There weren't any buckle bunnies—at least, none that I'd have liked to spend my life with."

There was silence as they both played with their spaghetti.

He tossed down his fork and gritted his teeth. "Amber, I could have helped you."

She shook her head. "It was my responsibility."

"Oh, for heaven's sake." He exhaled a loud breath. "Is your mom okay now?"

"No. It came back. She's going through chemo now." Tears stung her eyes. "Can we please change the subject? Let's go back to bull riding. It's mostly neutral.

"Yeah. Okay." Reed twirled his spaghetti with his fork. "How are your brothers doing? They have to be— what?—seniors in high school by now." He was still reeling. He hadn't known Mrs. Wainright had breast cancer again.

"The twins are great. They both got football scholarships. John is going to Notre Dame and Joe will be playing at the University of Southern California."

"Fabulous. I can't wait to see them play."

"They are both fans of yours. They're hoping you beat Luke for the championship in Vegas."

"So do I, but if I don't and he gets a fourth victory, it'll be a record that'll stand for a long time. That is, until I beat it." He laughed. "Jesse will ride the best he can, too. Maybe he'll be the one who'll beat Luke. But, as the saying goes, one cowboy against one bull."

She smiled slightly. "One cowboy against one bull. And one woman against one bull rider. I have to get back to work. I can't be playing all the time." She paused for several uncomfortable seconds. "And Reed, I think we should maintain a business relationship only. No more personal questions."

Reed raised an eyebrow. "Every woman I know likes to talk about herself."

Callie shook her head. "I don't."

"I guess I stand corrected," he said. "We'll limit our conversation to sex, drugs and rock and roll, but not if it pertains to ourselves."

"Exactly." Callie nodded.

"Okay," he said. "Then let's talk about sex."

CALLIE PUSHED AROUND a piece of chicken on her plate and wondered what on earth she should do.

But she didn't want to bare her soul to Reed. She'd done that way too many times with other men.

She'd told herself that she was going to take a break from men, and she'd meant it, and that included the amiable and happy-go-lucky Reed Beaumont.

Maybe she was only rowing with one oar, but she was going to stick to her promise to herself: concentrate on her business. Maybe someday she'd get her dream of going back to college.

"What did you say, Reed?"

"You look a million miles away."

"I guess I was," she said. "I guess I was just thinking."

"I don't suppose you'd care to share."

"No. It was nothing important. And it wasn't about sex."

Maybe indirectly it was about sex or lack thereof.

Callie was glad when Darlene returned with their take-out boxes and plastic bags. Callie put what was left of her meal into the containers. Reed did the same.

"This is going to be breakfast tomorrow," he said, and Callie believed him. Inez, the cook at the Beaumont Ranch, had just left for vacation.

Al returned, wiping his hands on his apron. "I always think when I work, and I think that you both are perfect together. So, let me show you my new reception halls."

Reed looked at Callie and raised an eyebrow. "Shall we, darling?"

Callie wasn't amused.

"Uh… Al…we have only become reacquainted for—" he checked his watch "—about three hours so far. As much as I like Callie, I don't want to rush things. Right, honey pie, my sweetheart darling?"

She tried not to laugh, she really did, but Reed always had a way of making her heart feel lighter, happier.

"Well, my beloved, I think we should leave before Al has us picking out a menu for our reception," Callie joked.

"Maybe we need to pick out rings first!"

"First, you need to go down on one knee," she instructed.

"I can't. I have a torn meniscus."

Callie looked up at the ceiling, painted with a landscape of Venice's Grand Canal with more gondolas than people. The artist loved his gondolas.

"We'd better go, Reed. I am way behind on my work today."

She started walking quickly, wanting to leave all the proposal, ring and reception talk behind.

Reed cleared his throat. "Ah, the real Callie returns. Nose-to-grindstone."

She was going to say something snooty in return but Reed was shaking hands with Al and she remembered her manners.

Walking back, she said, "Thanks, Al. Another great meal." She held out her hand, but he wrapped her in a hug instead. "Oh, we forgot our doggie boxes, Reed. I'll go get them."

She picked up the bags containing their leftover meals and couldn't resist peeking into the two rooms labeled Room A and Room B. They'd be perfect for an elegant wedding reception.

Hurrying back, she walked to the parking lot with Reed, and they got into Callie's SUV.

Reed chuckled. "You're not the only one who's going to be busy. Onward to the Beaumont Ranch, please. I have a lot of calls to make to find contractors."

"And I have a lot of paperwork to handle and file."

Callie had an excellent reputation for doing quality work, but it wouldn't hurt to give it more of a boost. She could raise her fees after working for the Beaumonts; their positive endorsement of her skills would get around the small town like wildfire.

"Can we share Big Dan's study?" Reed asked.

It *was* his father's study, after all, so she had no right to keep him out of the room. Wait a minute! The brothers had bought the ranch at a tax auction because Big Dan hadn't paid the taxes and had ignored the upkeep after

Valerie Lynn's death. So, Reed owned one-third of the ranch and the study was his, too.

"We could share the study on a trial basis," Callie said, turning left onto Rabbit Run Road. "If we can't work together, I can pack up everything and move someplace else and just go in there to file."

"But, Callie, we can get along. After all, we are faux engaged."

"And faux engaged is all that we'll ever be."

He raised an eyebrow. "Oh, yeah?"

"Yeah!"

"Is that some kind of a challenge for me to ask you out?" Reed asked.

"No. It is not. No way. Please don't misunderstand me. I'm not flirting with you. I'm telling you straight. I'm not interested in developing a relationship with you, Reed, or any man. Not at all. I've struck out way too many times."

Chapter Three

Callie was as prickly as a saguaro cactus. Reed should take the hint and stay away, but instead he was going to enjoy the challenge of getting to know her all over again.

In senior year of high school, he had fallen in love with the shy girl who was always ready with a smile and a laugh, but this Callie had ten years of secrets that had etched worry lines on her forehead. He planned on finding out what had caused them. And he wanted to bring laughter into her life again.

Or was he just being a fool and trying to salvage a relationship that was in the dreams of an eighteen-year-old?

Right now, he was thinking of an excuse to go to his father's study to look for something, or to ask her something, or to maybe bring her a glass of iced tea.

He went into the kitchen and looked into the fridge. Inez had made a pitcher of iced tea, bless her.

Finding a glass with a snap-on top, he tossed some ice into it, poured in the tea and put the container into a plastic grocery bag. Then he made his way into the study.

He found Callie sitting cross-legged on the floor, surrounded by papers and envelopes. There were two pens stuck into her hair and a pair of glasses on her head. Another pair was on her face. She was chewing on a pencil.

"Callie?"

She was concentrating so hard that she didn't appear to hear him.

"Callie, how about some iced tea?"

He'd spoiled her concentration. "Huh?"

"Iced tea. I brought you some." He held up the bag.

"Thanks. I need a break."

"I'm not staying," he said. "I didn't mean to interrupt you.

Oh, yes, I did!

He made his way to the big maroon leather chair he remembered his dad sitting in, smoking a cigar and barking orders. Big Dan's booming voice hadn't scared even the most timid of their help. His big smile and even bigger cigar were always present.

Fortunately, after three barroom brawls, Big Dan had been sentenced to probation and ordered into inpatient rehab for his alcohol problem. That had brought his drinking and gambling to a screeching halt, with a couple of relapses thrown in just to keep everyone on their toes.

Someday his dad would be back sitting in his chair just like before. Or maybe Big Dan would like to keep his apartment in town since every inch of the ranch reminded him of how he'd lost the love of his life.

After Hurricane Daphne hit, many historically accurate repairs of the ranch house and outbuildings had taken place under his brother Luke's watch. Unfortunately, Luke had ignored some of the mail and invoices, having much more pressing things on his mind, like bailing the ranch out of foreclosure.

"Um, Reed?"

Lost in thought, he didn't realize that Callie had her hand on the plastic bag with the container of iced tea and he wasn't giving it up.

"Oh, sorry. I was thinking of something."

"Big Dan's study is bringing back memories, isn't it?"

She could read him like good ol' Cowabunga—Cowabunga always knew if Reed was on his game or could be bucked off.

"Callie, you take Dad's chair. I'll sit in the brown leather one. That's where I always had to sit when he was lecturing or dishing out some kind of punishment."

He sank into the chair. He remembered the smell of leather, the sun shining in through the window and making patches on the carpet, and the swirl of the dust motes.

The room still smelled faintly of cigar smoke. As a kid, he'd both hated and loved that scent. It meant one of two things: that his father was nearby and some kind of punishment was headed his way, or it meant that his father was nearby and was going to do something fun with his brothers and him.

"How are you doing, Callie?" Looking around at the cluttered room, he realized what a dumb question that was. "I hate to tell you, but this office is looking worse, with all the assorted papers and envelopes on the floor."

She took a sip of iced tea. "It'll get worse before it gets better. I'm sorting."

"I see. Need help?"

Then Reed saw the perfect way to keep him near Callie when he wasn't busy hiring contractors: he could answer his own fan mail. He had a stack of unsigned pictures he could autograph and some nice paper with his letterhead. He could write a quick note to the fan.

"No. But thanks, anyway. I'm making progress," she said, waving her hand in dismissal.

He looked at the now six bags full of mail. He never realized that he and his brothers had all those fans.

"I think I should answer my own fan mail, Callie. I

feel bad that I neglected them. I'm going to write a note and send a signed picture."

He repeated himself. "Yes. It's time I answered my own fan mail."

Callie grunted. "I could set you up in the kitchen. Or your bedroom. You could answer it there."

"Why bother? I have everything here that I need."

"Reed, I see what you're doing. You want to pester me and drive me crazy."

"Nah. I have better things to do. Besides, you made it crystal clear—I think those were the words you used— that you weren't interested in me. So I don't see a problem. Pretend I'm not here in my own father's study."

"Reed—" He felt like her eyes were throwing daggers at his chest.

He grinned. "I think you're protesting way too much. I can only think that you have feelings for me."

"Just wait until I show you how wrong you are, cowboy."

EARLY IN THE morning on her second day of work, Callie received a call from the brothers' agent.

"Reed, I have to talk to you," she said, waiting for the sound of his crutches. He was in the expansive ranch house somewhere. "Reed?"

"At your service, ma'am." He was in the kitchen reading the paper and chugging coffee.

"Rick would like to know if you could fill in for one of his other clients. They want you to cook with a celebrity chef."

He shrugged. "When and where?"

"This afternoon. They will come here to you. The show is called *What's in Your Refrigerator?*"

"That sounds easy enough. What are we going to cook?"

"Whatever they find in your fridge. They are going to make a meal out of it."

"Interesting concept," he joked.

"Can you cook, Reed?"

He shrugged his shoulders. "No, I can't. But I'm a master with a microwave."

"If they use a microwave, I'd be surprised."

"You never know." He smiled. "Maybe I'll go shine it up. Then I'm going to see what Inez left in the fridge before she went on vacation."

"No. I had to promise that you wouldn't open it until they tell you to do so on the air."

He held up his hands in surrender. "I shall not open it then. I don't want to be arrested by the fridge police."

"Good."

"What a bull rider has to do, huh?" he asked.

"Probably with all the publicity you are getting, you'll get new fans, and then there'll be new fans for the PBR. The money doesn't hurt, either. Your product endorsements are very lucrative, too."

"The Three Musketeers are putting most every cent we can into the ranch."

Callie nodded. "I can tell you are all pitching in, from some of the bank statements I've seen."

"You're going to know all about us, except what size underwear we wear."

"Oh, I found a receipt from the Beaumont Emporium. I know that, too."

He looked at Callie, eyes as wide as some of the belt buckles he sported.

She laughed. "Only kidding."

He laughed. She enjoyed how he laughed—free and easy—as if he didn't have a care in the world.

In fact, that was the essence of his personality. It must be nice to be like that.

"Reed, can I make a suggestion?"

"Try and stop you."

"I think you should wear your cowboy clothes. Cargo shorts and a T-shirt that says Beach Bum might not be what this show is looking for."

"Point taken. I'll be right back." He hurried down the hallway.

Callie wondered if Reed's room was the same as it was in high school. She remembered it as a cheery room with colorful Navajo blankets and shelves packed with trophies and belt buckles. Each award displayed a picture of the presenter and the name of the event. There were bigger pictures of saddles, rifles and boots that he'd won—more boots than a man could ever wear. No wonder that they always looked like he'd just taken them out of a box. He had.

Several minutes later, the doorbell rang, and Reed yelled, "Do you mind getting that, Callie?"

"No problem." She put down the files she was labeling on a cleared spot on the big desk and headed for the door.

"Hi," she said, looking at all the equipment several people were unloading from a van parked out front.

An older woman with a clipboard waved. "We're from *What's in Your Refrigerator?*"

"Come in," Callie said. "I'll show you where the kitchen is and you can set up."

A man with a white chef's jacket and black-and-white-checked pants whistled. "I am Chef Marty. What a fabulous place! I heard that it was historic, but this is amazing."

"Hello, Chef Marty. I'm Callie, assistant for the Beaumont family. The ranch really is a historic place. It was founded at the time of the Oklahoma Land Rush." Callie grinned. "The founder, Daniel Beaumont, was said to be a Sooner. He was Reed's great-grandfather, times a few greats."

She thought she sounded like a tour guide, but she had grown up in the light of one of the most historical places in Oklahoma. Every man, woman and child in Beaumont knew the story of the old place.

"It's totally ancient. It's totally medieval," said a kid in sunglasses lugging an aluminum suitcase and with an e-cigarette in his mouth; she thought he was probably an intern.

"Not quite medieval," Reed said, entering in the kitchen. "But close."

"Excuse me, I have work to do," Callie said, hurrying back to the study. As much as she would like to ogle Reed, she was better off away from him. Their earlier exchange had been a lot of fun, as was any time they talked together, but she needed to focus on her job.

She supposed she could stretch her duties to make sure everything was going smoothly in the kitchen, but what could go wrong?

Thump! Boom!

Someone swore.

Then three more people swore.

"Dude, are you okay?"

Callie went running. In her gut, she knew what had happened: Reed had lost his balance.

Oh, no! She hoped that he hadn't hurt his knee even more.

But it wasn't Reed on the ground. It was a crock of chili that Inez had made before she left that had hit the thick tiles and splashed all over Reed, the chef and the lady and her clipboard.

"Dude, this is epic," said the kid with the sunglasses.

"I'll double down on that," Reed said.

Callie sprang into action. She grabbed a roll of paper towels and began scooping the chili into a trash can.

As best as he could, Reed tried to help her. None of the TV people lifted a finger, and that annoyed her.

"Reed, you can't kneel down with your problems. I'll take care of this while you change your jeans."

"I hate to stick you with cleaning up."

"I have twin brothers who play high school football, baseball and basketball. Can you guess at how many things hit the floor? They're always tossing something, bouncing something or knocking over something with some kind of ball."

"You're too good. My mother would have made us clean it up," Reed said.

"Oh, I do. Then I clean it up much better after they're finished." She turned toward Chef Marty. "Is it still a go for the show?"

"Absolutely. It looks like we are going to make grilled ham and cheese using flour tortillas. Then we are going to make salsa."

"I think Reed can handle that," Callie said.

While the TV crew took a break outside, Callie found a mop and bucket in the walk-in pantry and mopped the area. Then she dried it with more paper towels.

"I can't thank you enough, Callie."

She jumped at the low but familiar voice. Puffs of air teased her neck as he whispered close to her ear. Turning, she noticed that Reed had changed into black jeans that clung perfectly in all the right places, along with a long-sleeved white shirt covered with either embroidery or sewed-on patches of products and companies that sponsored him.

He had changed his boots from brown to black—alligator, maybe, or some kind of snake.

Not that she'd noticed.

"Oh, uh…you're welcome," she said, managing to look away from Reed. "Well, I'd better get back to work."

"I'll take you out for your kindness, Callie. I won't forget." Reed turned, probably knowing she'd protest. "Let's get this show back to the kitchen and get cooking."

She couldn't help it. She had to watch him walk—crutch—away.

Callie had to get away from Reed, the scent of chili and the young kid with the e-cigarette that smelled like bubble gum.

She couldn't wait to return to the pounds of paper that divulged the financial secrets of the Beaumonts and get everything entered on her spreadsheet.

CALLIE SURE WAS a good sport, Reed thought. Whatever Luke was paying her, it wasn't enough. She was even cleaning up chili explosions. It didn't go unnoticed that the rest of the people in the kitchen hadn't lifted a finger to help, except for the young dude with the sunglasses who'd kept handing Callie paper towels. His name was Arnold and, as it turned out, he was the director of the show.

Reed, who had been feeling every ache and pain lately that came from riding bulls, really felt like an elder statesman of the bull-riding world when he realized he had saddles older than Arnie.

"Let's get going, ladies and gentlemen," Reed said. "My knee and lack of intact ligaments are killing me."

Arnie blew a whistle, which made them all flinch.

No one was talking, so the loud sound made it all the more bizarre. "Let's move it, people. Our bull-riding star is faltering."

"Not faltering, Arnie. Just aching," Reed clarified. "If I faltered, I could never ride."

Maybe he should just get the darn surgery and get rid of the crutches and stop wasting time.

So far, in his career, he'd managed to escape surgery. Oh, he'd had broken bones that had needed to be set and shoulders that had needed to be jammed back to where they belonged and petty stuff like that, but he'd never had real hospital surgery.

The saying went, "When you're a bull rider, it's *when*—and not *if*—you'll get hurt." He'd had his share of problems, but a lot of riders had had it a lot worse.

Chef Marty now had him grating Colby cheese.

"Do you have cilantro?" asked the chef.

"I'll look in Inez's garden," Reed said.

"Can't you send your secretary out there to get the stuff?" asked Arnie.

Reed raised his eyes to the ceiling. "Callie is *not* my secretary—she's an administrative assistant and a very successful businesswoman, and I think she's done enough to help us out here. I'll get the cilantro, and Chef Marty can keep chopping."

"No!" whined Arnie. "You have to do the chopping, bull rider dude."

"Reed."

Arnie looked around. "What's that?"

"That's my name," Reed said. "I am *not* a dude. Well, I am a dude, but that's not my name."

"Oh. Yeah. I know, dude... I mean Reed. My secretary, uh...um—my administrative assistant—" He snapped his fingers. "Louella. Louella will get it."

Callie must have heard her name earlier because she walked into the kitchen with a handful of cilantro.

"I thought it would speed things up if I got the cilantro," she whispered to Reed as she handed the greenery to the chef.

"That means I owe you two nights out," Reed said.

Callie motioned with her head for him to follow her, and she picked a quiet spot away from the TV people. "That means that when everyone leaves, I can have some quiet time to work."

Reed raised an eyebrow. "You don't want to go out with me? How about tonight?"

"Reed, thanks for asking, but I don't have time. Tonight I have to go to my brothers' baseball game, and I have some housework to do. Besides, I have other clients to handle other than the Beaumonts. So, no. I can't go out with you. Thank you, anyway."

"I'll take you to your brothers' game." Callie was just about to say no when Reed added, "They're open to the public, right?"

"You know they are."

"Meet you there."

"But you can't drive, Reed."

"Oh. That's right." He rubbed his chin. "If it's not too much trouble, would you pick me up?"

"You're… You…you are incorrigible!" She stared at him without blinking. "And this will not, I repeat *not*, be a date."

Her constant rejection would have made any other man give up on her, but there was a reason for it, and he didn't think that it all had to do with him.

When the occasion presented itself, he was going to find out what had made her so vehemently against dating him.

While the others were huddled around a monitor of some sort, Reed went into the study to retrieve his wallet. At the same time, Callie's cell phone, which she'd left on Big Dan's desk, rang and she hurried to answer it.

"Hi, Mom. I was just going to call you. How are you feeling?…Uh-huh. Feeling well enough to go to the twins' baseball game?" She paused. "Okay, great! I'll meet you at the high school then…Yes, save an extra seat…Yes, um, it's for Reed Beaumont…No, Mom, it's nothing like that. He just wanted to go…I don't know why—he just does—so just save another seat if you get there before I do."

Callie clicked her cell phone off and slipped it into her purse.

"Callie, I couldn't help but overhearing… Is your mother doing okay?"

She took a deep breath and then let it out.

"I'm sorry. I didn't mean to pry, but it sounded like you were worried. I know the feeling. My father has me worried most of the time."

He gave a half-hearted smile. "I remember your mother from when she was our school nurse in grammar school. I remember how she was always making sure that everyone had all their shots, and she always sent get-well cards when we had to stay home with one of those childhood diseases. I got them all—measles, mumps and chicken pox—and I received several more cards from her."

"Mom has breast cancer again. She's doing chemo. Doc Lansing feels that she'll beat it this time, too. But I'm scared, Reed. The chemo is hitting her hard this time. She always hates to lose her hair, so she has a bunch of wigs. She'd have to be really bad before she missed one of the twins' games. She went to all of them—football, baseball and basketball—unless she was horribly ill. Mom and I were so grateful when they got football scholarships. I couldn't afford to send them to college." She took a deep breath and looked at Reed. "What is it about you that makes me just spill my guts? I usually keep my life to myself."

"Maybe I'm a good listener."

"I think that's probably true."

Reed reached out to take Callie's hand but then changed his mind. He thought that she wouldn't welcome the contact. "Or maybe you're just feeling overwhelmed. I mean, just look at this mess. I feel like I should help you more, not only just answering my fan mail."

"I hired on for this job, Reed. It means everything to me. With the Beaumont account, I'll be in more demand and I can provide for my family more.

"Good for you." Reed knew how she felt, being able to help her family, and admired her to no end. He'd had the same feelings when he was able to help save his family's ranch from both the auction block and Hurricane Daphne. Well, actually, the Daphne work continued.

"Hey! Hey, bull rider, Reed! Are you ready to begin again?" Arnie's usually thin voice was exceptionally loud. "Let's get going, please."

Callie smiled. "Cowboy up, Reed. The cooking show must go on."

He was reluctant to leave her when they'd had a good conversation going. "I'm making grilled ham and cheese on a tortilla with fresh salsa. If I don't burn everything, we can eat what I make. So, how about dining with me before the game?"

Callie looked like she knew when she was beat. "Okay, cowboy. I'll dine with you."

Finally!

Reed chuckled. "Can we call it a date?"

"No!"

"I'm going to keep asking you, Callie. From what I can tell, you seem to need a little fun in your life."

Her usually lush lips transformed into a thin white line. "And you're just the cowboy to provide the fun, huh?"

"I can try."

"You can try, but you won't get far."

Reed winked. "We'll see about that."

ABOUT AN HOUR LATER, just when she was getting into designing a spreadsheet, Callie's cell phone rang. She saw that it was Big Dan's probation officer, Matty Matthews. Matty had been two years ahead of her in high school and was coached her brothers in basketball.

"Matty Matthews? This is Callie Wainright. Which one of my brothers got hurt this time?"

He chuckled. "Neither. They are both alive and kicking, but I have a favor to ask you."

She sat and tried to calm her thumping heart. "Name it."

"Big Dan isn't concentrating on his rehab, Callie. He's too damn distracted. He needs someone to take care of depositing his Social Security check. I'd do it, but office rules state we can't take money from probationers. Oh, and Big Dan also wants someone to take periodic pictures of the ranch so he can see the progress made, but actually, Callie, I think he just wants someone to talk to him about the outside world—mostly about what his boys are doing. I have over a hundred probationers on my roster. I can't be at Dan's beck and call."

"I'm sure Reed's going to feel like he should have this responsibility if he could drive, but until then, I'd be glad to help out." She wrote diligently on a notebook page: *deposit Social Sec check, talk, take pictures of ranch, etc.*

"Oh…and, Callie?"

"Yes, Matty?"

"Could you possibly get Reed to come up and see him, please? He's at the Beaumont County Alcohol and Drug Rehabilitation Facility. He needs company. Big Dan is about to go ballistic."

"I'm sure that Reed has been meaning to see Big Dan, but there's been a lot of going on lately. I'll be sure to pass along your message."

Soon after they hung up, Callie realized she had just become the personal assistant to Big Dan Beaumont.

Callie was ready to explode with happiness. With the extra income, she could pay more money on her mortgage, keep up with monthly insurance premiums and add an extra payment on medical bills for her whole family and herself. Maybe she could even save for a new car.

And get a bachelor's degree.

That had always been her dream. "Maybe someday, it'll be my turn," she mumbled to herself.

Until then, she was going to work as hard as possible to do a great job for the Beaumont family, and to keep Reed, his charming demeanor, killer good looks and quirky sense of humor at bay.

She had to focus intently if she wanted to expand her business and keep it growing.

And Reed couldn't help her unless he stayed away from her completely.

Chapter Four

"Callie, everyone's gone and dinner's ready!" Reed yelled from the kitchen.

She got up from Big Dan's chair and walked into the kitchen. The table was set with a lone votive candle, two glasses of what looked like iced tea, and the ham and cheese tortillas.

"Looks good, Reed. How does it taste?"

"It's not bad at all," Reed said. "It's better warm and all gooey. If it gets cold, it tastes like concrete, so I microwaved this for thirty seconds in a paper towel. We'll have to eat fast before they turn."

Laughing, Callie took a seat opposite Reed at the huge dark table. The table had at least fourteen matching, high-backed chairs. This was a table for a large family, a family that liked to entertain. That was the Beaumonts. Their dinner parties were legendary, as were their rodeos and bull-riding events at the arena at the front of their property.

A stab of jealousy went through Callie whenever she saw a family working, playing and going to church together. Her mother had tried to be both parents, but her health hadn't let her. So Callie had stepped in, raised her brothers and held her mother's hand through chemo.

Her mother had loved the annual Beaumont rodeo

and barbecue. Just about the whole town turned out for a weekend of fun. Sometimes, her mother was too weak to go, but she put on her wig, and Callie wheeled her to the event.

Luckily, Hurricane Daphne had spared the arena—mostly—and the first rodeo since Valerie Lynn had died had been held last year with Luke leading the charge,

Her mother had been well enough to attend, so they'd all squished together in Callie's ancient car and headed for the Beaumont ranch. Her mother had put on her wig and Callie had wheeled her to the event.

Callie had convinced herself that she should talk to Reed, but there were always so many people around him all the time, she'd never had the opportunity. If the conditions had been right, she might have even worked up the courage, or maybe not.

Callie'd told herself she wasn't afraid of how Reed might react to her, not at all; she'd just wanted the right time to approach him. She'd thought that, after all these years, she should just work up the courage to pull him away from his entourage and fans and ask him for a private moment.

She took a bite of Reed's creation. "It's pretty good, Reed." She took another bite and knew he was right. It was turning into concrete.

"Callie, I still wish you had come with me when we graduated. We could have seen the world together."

She shook her head. "How would we have seen the world, Reed? One day at each bull-riding event, before we had to drive to the next one, isn't seeing the world, Reed. It's zigzagging across the country." She put the tortilla down. "Why do you want to rehash this? I wasn't ready to leave Beaumont, that's all. Besides, I had responsibilities at home."

"Don't you ever have fun anymore? Do a little boot scootin'? Throw back some cold ones? Run away with a cowboy?" He winked.

Her mouth went dry, and she reached for her water glass. If he only knew how many times she wished that she'd run away with him.

"I know you're joking, but thanks, anyway. I have a company to run and clients who aren't Beaumonts to tend to." Callie sipped some water.

"Would you like me to heat up your tortilla?" Reed asked.

"Don't move. I can do it myself."

"But you're my guest."

"But you're injured and I'm not your guest. I work here."

She slid her plate into the microwave and waited for ten seconds. That ought to revive it. She normally wouldn't bother, but she was hungry, and she had a football game to watch.

She might as well explain more. "I knew you were hurt when I wouldn't go with you, but put yourself in my place. I had to stay here and work. You know that my father was a gambler—*is* a gambler. The whole town knows it still. We were evicted out of every house we rented because Mom was sick and couldn't work. If you recall, I was working at the diner as a waitress after school. That was our only money coming in. My brothers were too young to work then." She paused for a breath. "Please don't think I'm whining, Reed, or complaining. I'm just stating fact.

"I understand," he said solemnly. "Go on. You never told me this."

"One of my graduation presents was yet another eviction for nonpayment of rent—*all* the rent. My hours at

Beaumont Pizza were cut back because the state fair was on and business was slow. My other graduation present was my father running off to Tahiti with Tish Holcomb. The story goes that they met on a gambling cruise. Yes, my father, Melvin Wainright, managed to get on a cruise to Tahiti while his wife, my poor mother, was having chemo for breast cancer. He left her. Left us."

"Where's he now?"

"According to one of his friends, he's still in Tahiti with Tish. Apparently she hasn't run out of money yet."

"I'm so sorry, Callie. I knew you were dealing with most of that. You never told me the details."

"I was too embarrassed. Believe me, Reed. I would have given anything to go with you, but I couldn't leave. My twin brothers were seven at the time and Mom was too sick to corral them. It fell to me. I was exhausted most of the time, and was way out of my element, but I did it."

"No wonder you couldn't leave."

"I wanted to. Oh, how I wanted to. I just couldn't."

"I just wanted to spend my life with you, Callie. I just know you were the one, and I figured that we could make it work somehow."

"If I had gone with you, where would we have lived? In your pickup truck? Where would we have settled down?"

"When I started winning, I could have towed a trailer."

Callie sighed. "How would I have known that you would have started winning? It would have been a gamble, Reed, and even though my father is a gambler, I am not."

"I never had any doubt."

"And I had nothing but doubts." She looked into his deep blue eyes. "Reed, after all those evictions, I have to have a home. A permanent one. I bought the house that we are living in on Elm Street. It's mine. Well, it's the bank's, but since I bought it, we haven't been evicted— ever. I need a permanent place in which to live. It's important to me."

He was silent, as if he was mulling over what she'd just said.

He put his hand over hers. "Callie, I really wish you had explained all this before. I wouldn't have spent ten years trying to convince myself that I hated you."

Her heart pounded faster. She needed to get away from his blue eyes, away from the magnificent ranch that had seen its own share of sorrow and away from the sad smile on Reed's face.

As Reed folded himself into Callie's SUV, he stole a glance at her.

Dammit! He had to be the most selfish cowboy on the face of the planet.

Why hadn't she told him? He would have understood much better than the "I just have obligations" speech. Or would he have? At the age of eighteen, with his fresh PBR card in his hand, a list of events and a new pickup for his graduation, he'd been geared up and invincible.

Everything had been perfect, except that he'd wanted Callie by his side, always.

Maybe she'd been right by not going with him. Life was tough on the road and there was little time for sightseeing. He spent most of his time in arena after arena, at various fairgrounds and even parking lots.

In between, he would ride practice bulls at the ranches of his fellow riders, at the practice arenas of stock contractors and wherever else he was invited.

He trained, signed autographs, did whatever his advertisers wanted him to do, and he partied with his fellow riders.

In retrospect, Callie would have been bored. He was never bored. He spent every free moment he had working out and becoming a better bull rider. He'd wanted to prove to Callie how wrong she was by not going with him.

He was never without female admirers, and he dated frequently, but none of them were Callie.

She turned into Beaumont High's parking lot and they got out of her SUV. Kickoff was about to start, so they stopped on the sidelines of the football field to watch.

The other team got the ball, so Callie motioned for him to follow her to the bleachers. She took them to the second row. Mrs. Wainright was there, wearing a glittery red-rhinestone baseball cap.

Callie and Reed slid in next to her.

"Hi, Reed. It's been a long time." She lifted her hand to shake his. Her grip was weak and he was careful not to squeeze her hand hard at all. Sadly, she looked thin and frail, not at all like the vigorous and healthy woman that he remembered.

He felt bad for Callie and the boys, too. When a loved one went through a sickness, everyone went through it.

"Yes, Mrs. Wainright. It *has* been a long time." He didn't know what to say next, but she helped him out.

"Reed, I think you're old enough to call me Connie." She smiled, still gripping his hand.

"Okay, um, uh… Con… I mean Mrs. Wainright." He laughed. "You know, I just can't call you Connie. You'll always be Mrs. Wainright, school nurse. With you, we couldn't get away with anything!"

"Damn straight." She laughed but the effort seemed to pain her. She shifted on the bleacher seat. "And you and your pals tried everything in the book to get out of school. Too bad you didn't put that energy into your work."

"Yes, Mrs. Wa-in-right," Reed answered in a child's singsong voice.

Connie laughed until she began to cough. She pulled out a bottle of water from a tote bag, opened the cap and took a couple of sips.

"There's Joe and John." Callie jumped up, cupped her mouth with her hands, and yelled to them. "Yeah… Wainrights! Go, Bobcats, go! Yeah, team!"

Reed knew that the Beaumont Bobcats were well known in the Oklahoma high school circuit for their basketball, football and rodeo teams.

"Callie, are your brothers on the rodeo team, too?"

"No. That's one thing that they never had an interest in. Probably because we don't own a ranch and they haven't been exposed to horses and bulls and cattle and the like. Thank goodness." She waved her hand in front of her face like a fan. Then she whispered to herself, "Yes, thank goodness. I can't afford any more insurance bills, and I don't want them hurt. I worry about you getting hurt all the time, too, Reed." She pointed to his knee. "Know what I mean?"

"It's nice to know that you worry about me."

Every time she'd watched Reed ride, she'd held her breath for eight seconds.

"I just want everyone to be safe. With my brothers, football, baseball and basketball are their sports, but they like football the best. I told you they received full scholarships. That's a blessing."

"Very impressive. Notre Dame and USC. They didn't want to go the same school?"

"No," Mrs. Wainright answered. "They thought that

they should have their own identities in college. They said they were tired of being called the Wainright Twins. But I don't have a doubt in my mind that they will miss one another."

Callie put her hand on her mother's shoulder. "And we'll miss them terribly, won't we, Mom?"

"We sure will."

Joe was ready to kick the ball for three points and Callie whistled and called his name. Then she remained silent and held her breath. She knotted her hands together and gripped them tightly. Mrs. Wainright remained silent, her eyes never leaving the field. Callie looked like she was going to burst. That is, until Joe scored right over the goal post.

Later, when John had the football and was sprinting across the field toward the posts, Callie repeated the same ritual. This time, mother and daughter gripped hands. Automatically, Callie reached for Reed's hand.

Reed looked down at their hands. Her hands were delicate and smooth. His were rough and callused from bull riding. She wore a pale green-stoned ring that had drifted to the side. He moved it back in place with a finger.

This was what he liked—holding Callie's hand. He felt comfortable in Callie's little family and seeing how much she adored her mother reminded him of his own family, too. It was times like this when he missed his mother, and his father, too. Maybe someday, Dan would come around. Without taking her eyes from the game, Callie quietly said, "Green peridot from Arizona. Birthstone. August."

Callie gripped his hand tighter as her brother was outrunning the other team and was mere feet from the end zone.

As hard as she gripped, Callie could never beat the

strength of a bull rope, sticky with rosin, wrapped around his fingers and wedged into the handle. He liked the feeling. But feeling Callie's soft hand in his, well…he could stay like this forever.

Suddenly, Callie let out a scream that would send a herd of buffalos over in Yellowstone running for Canada. As John scored, Callie jumped up and down on the bleachers and screamed even more. They still held hands.

Reed saw that Mrs. Wainright had sat down, smiling and out of breath. When it seemed she noticed their clenched hands, she raised an eyebrow, smiled at Reed and nodded as if she approved. She then excused herself and mumbled something about the concession stand.

"Okay, Mom."

Callie raised her hand and Reed's came with it. She stared, her eyes opening wide in surprise. Then she frowned and pulled away. He half expected her to wipe her palm on her jeans.

"Oh. Sorry," she said softly. "When did you—"

"Oh, no, sweetheart. You grabbed my hand first."

"I didn't."

"Oh, yes, you did. And there's no need to apologize." Reed quirked an eyebrow and whispered, "Was it good for you?"

The corners of her mouth turned up in a smile and he wondered what it would be like feel those luscious lips pressed against his again.

She rolled her eyes.

Reed rubbed his hands together as if proud of himself. "I still got it, don't I?"

She took a deep breath. "I'd bet that you never lost it."

"Care to find out?"

CALLIE PUT HER hands on her hips. "Quit flirting with me, Reed. I don't have the time for such craziness."

He stared into her eyes. "Where have I heard that before?"

"I know. I know. I've told you a million times, but it hasn't sunk in."

He took his hat off and pointed to his thick black hair with a touch of curl at the ends. "We bull riders have hard heads."

"Your head must be the hardest of all."

"Ouch." He raised a finger and pointed it at her. "You're the one who put your hand in mine. That's why we're having this discussion."

His eyes twinkled and the tone of his voice told her that he was kidding.

Two could play at this game.

"Reed, how would I know for sure that I took your hand first?"

"Because I said so, and I don't lie."

"But how would I know for sure?"

Reed turned his head up to the sky, as if praying. "There is no way to know for sure. I'm just asking you to believe me."

"Humph."

"Callie, we didn't have sex on these bleachers, for heaven's sake. We only held hands."

"And now my mother thinks we're dating."

"Your mother still approves of me dating you, and I like her. A lot. She's a courageous lady."

"She approves of... *What did you say?*"

"That she approves of me dating you. She nodded at me and grinned."

"Oh, for heaven's sake, is this a conspiracy against me? Read my lips—we are not dating, cowboy." She took a deep breath then let it out. "I'll talk to Mom. We'll sort this all out."

"There's nothing to sort out, Callie. You grabbed my hand in excitement." He rubbed her back. "I wonder what else you do when you're excited. Never mind, I remember."

His large hand was warm as his fingers traced a circle, small at first, then large, then back to small until he stopped. However he didn't remove it.

Callie sat motionless as the heat branded her back. She stole a glance at Reed, who was watching the game. Of all the time to watch a football game, this was not it.

The game faded from her sight and hearing. She tried not to notice the heat of his hand on her back, the smell of his aftershave, the closeness of his strong body.

One slight turn of her head and their lips would be touching. She had to break away and now, before things got too serious.

"Go, Wainrights! Yeah, Bobcats!" She jumped to her feet and yelled as loud as she possibly could, "Bobcats rule!" She expected that the thinning crowd would cheer along, but instead they all turned to stare at her.

Finally she looked at the field.

Empty.

The game was over and, according to the scoreboard, the Bobcats had lost by three points.

What was she doing? All she knew was that her mind wasn't where it should be and that Reed was driving her crazy.

Suddenly, Reed jumped to his feet and clapped. "Yeah, Bobcats! Great game, Bobcats! Go, Bobcats!"

Her savior.

She smiled at Reed in gratitude. Okay, maybe he wasn't such an inconvenience, and he was kind of fun to have around. He was right—she needed some fun—and he certainly was fun.

It would be so easy to fall for him again. Or maybe he'd always been there in the back of her mind. Maybe she couldn't give her all to her past relationships, and perhaps they realized that someone else was always in the back of her heart and mind.

And that someone was Reed.

She was so preoccupied that she didn't see her mother return to the bleachers.

"Reed, Callie, would you like to join us for ice cream at the Ice Palace?" she asked. "Most of the team is going and there's a blanket invitation to the fans."

"I really can't, Mom. I have way too much—"

"We'd love to join you," Reed said. "Callie was just saying that she's in the mood for ice cream."

"Great."

Callie raised an eyebrow. She should be mad that he was making decisions for her, but the thought of ice cream made her mouth water. "Sure, I'd love to go."

"I'll ride with your brothers and you two can go together, of course." Her mother giggled—and she never giggled. In spite of her health, she almost skipped away.

"I'm beginning to think that your mother is trying to get us together," Reed said.

Callie shook her head. "She wouldn't."

"Okay. Whatever you say."

Callie thought about how her mother had been acting during the game and had a sinking feeling in her stomach. "Oh, shoot. Maybe she is. I'll have a talk with her."

"Don't bother. It's kind of fun."

"It's not fun for me," Callie said.

"Callie—"

"Before you talk, I know you're going to tell me that

I should have more fun, but this is the kind that I can do without."

They started to walk to Callie's SUV, and she pointed. "Reed, how about if I drive the car closer to that bench over there? You must be getting tired with those crutches. Go sit down."

"I can walk it."

"Okay." She should have known. He was a tough bull rider.

By the time they reached her SUV, he was sweating and breathing hard.

He turned to Callie. "It's been a long day, my knee is killing me and I need a break from these crutches. I see what the doc means about putting my feet up."

"We can skip the ice cream and I'll take you home instead."

"But we agreed to go," he said. "I'll be okay as soon as I sit down for a while."

Callie could see the lines of pain on his forehead and she worried all over again for him. He was always so strong and to see a dent in his armor worried her. She opened the passenger-side door and held it open for him. Holding out her hand, she took his crutches, so he could get in.

"Thanks, Callie."

"No problem."

As she got into the SUV, she said, "Are you sure you are up for ice cream?"

"Large chocolate in a cone. No sprinkles."

She started the engine. "I'll get it for you. Anything else?"

"If you don't mind, I'd love a bottle of water. Ice cream always makes me thirsty."

"Me, too!" she said. "I wonder why."

"Beats me."

If an ice cream place could be an iconic location, the Ice Palace was the one in Beaumont. There was a big black-and-white plastic cow on the roof. The three windows for ordering were located in the base of a huge vanilla cone. The top of the cone was shaped like a huge mound of ice cream that ended in a point with a little drooping curlicue. It was…cute and left no doubt to the imagination as to what the place was selling.

Reed chuckled. "When I was a kid, and Big Dan was coaching, we used to go to the Ice Palace after every game. Some coaches took their players out when they won, but my father's thinking was that as long as we tried hard, we deserved ice cream."

"Good thinking on his part."

"Yeah. I've been putting off seeing him again. He's cranky and not like his old self. It's like a kick in the gut by a half-ton bull."

Callie sighed. "I'm really sorry about your dad. All of Beaumont liked Big Dan until…until…"

"Until he started boozing and fighting in bars?"

"Well, yes." She nodded, putting the SUV in gear. "How is he doing?"

"Big Dan is now Little Dan. He's a shadow of what he used to look like, but he's been doing okay in rehab. Matty Matthews is his probation officer, and he's keeping a tight rein on him, but Big Dan always manages to get leave and look the ranch over."

She snapped her fingers. "Oh, I forgot to tell you that Matty wants me to go to the bank for your father on occasion."

"I'm sorry, Callie. I could have done it if it wasn't for a certain bull who held a grudge for riding him in the past." Callie chuckled, turned out of the parking lot and aimed her SUV toward the Ice Palace.

Excitement shot through her. She didn't want the evening to end. Maybe she could use more fun in her life. And Reed was fun.

She arrived at the Ice Palace and found her brothers pointing to a parking space at the front. Smoothly, she pulled into it.

Callie opened the door then turned back to Reed. "You might want to sit here and relax. I'll stand in line."

"And miss all the fun? No way!" He exited the vehicle and hobbled over to stand at the back of the line.

"Hey, it's Reed Beaumont!"

Soon Reed was encircled by high schoolers and their parents. Pens and papers appeared for autographs. One tall redhead pulled up her T-shirt and wanted him to sign her tanned, flat stomach. Her navel was pierced with a diamond, winking at him, at everyone.

Was she ever that young and did she ever act that inappropriately?

"Sorry, honey. I don't sign body parts." He shook his head. As far as Callie was concerned, Reed just went up a rung on her ladder. Maybe three.

A huge man approached wearing a Sooners hoodie. "What's going on here, Lina?"

She smoothed her top down and walked backward a couple of feet. "Nothing, Daddy. I just wanted Reed Beaumont's autograph."

She was Lina Capria? Callie remembered babysitting her on occasion. How time flew!

Reed held out his hand to shake Lina's father's hand. "That's all we're doing here, sir. Talking. And I'm signing autographs for those who want one."

"Add one for me." He shook Reed's hand. "I'm a fan of yours. All of Beaumont is."

Callie dug in her purse, found a little spiral notebook and handed it to Reed.

He smiled at her, scribbled his name on one of the pages, tore it off and handed it to Lina. Then he signed one for her father.

"Thanks, Reed," Lina said, sending him a kiss through pursed lips. No wonder her father kept her on a short leash.

With that, father and daughter disappeared somewhere into another line.

Reed turned to Callie and whispered, "Do you have any body parts you'd like to have signed?"

"Nope."

Her mother, in the next line, waved her over.

"I'll be right back, Reed. I'm going to talk to my mother."

He nodded and went back to talking to his fans.

"Callie, I just wanted to tell you that it's good to good to see you dating again, honey."

"I'm not dating, Mom. It's not a good time for me."

"Reed is still perfect for you. I always thought that you two should get together."

"Oh, Mom." She didn't want to discuss her dating life—or lack thereof—with her mother.

"I've always liked Reed."

"Mom, you've liked every man that I've dated."

"No. Reed's different." She put a hand on Callie's shoulder. "Honey, I want grandchildren while I'm still able to enjoy them."

Callie would like nothing better than to have a bunch of kids, but she wanted to find the right man to raise them with her. It wasn't Mike McBride, Noah Young or Jack Cummings, that's for sure.

Was Reed that man?

Chapter Five

"Reed, uh…did you arrive with my sister?" Joe Wainright asked, as soon as Reed's fans disbursed.

"I was just going to ask the same question," John Wainright said.

Reed could tell them apart only because their first names were embroidered on the visors of their ball caps.

The Wainright Twins stood in front of him, a six-foot-three-inch wall of athletic strength. They'd do well playing college football.

"Your sister has been driving me around. I can't drive, so she's been helping me. You might say, too, that I am one of her clients in her business. We went to the game, and then your mother invited us for ice cream. Is there a problem?"

"Callie has been hurt, dude," John said. "A lot."

"We don't want her hurt anymore," added Joe.

"Listen, I don't plan on hurting Callie. I know you love her, but here's where I tell you to butt out. Enough said?"

The brothers looked at each other and something passed between them. Joe turned to him. "Yeah. Enough said."

Reed held out his hand and, without hesitation, they each took it and shook. It seemed as though the brothers had accepted him, but they had let him know that they were keeping an eye on him. He'd do the same, if he'd had a sister. Then they went back to their teammates.

A space became available at a picnic table and Reed sat and waited.

Finally, Callie arrived and handed him a large chocolate ice cream on a cone. He took a long lick.

"Yee-haw!" he said. "Delicious. It's been a long time since I've had Ice Palace chocolate. I've gone to other places in my travels, but this stuff is the best. I'm addicted to their ice cream."

Callie had a bowl of vanilla loaded with colorful sprinkles. "It *is* divine."

"I wish I could order this wherever I'm riding."

"You can't. You'd have to move back to Beaumont to get it."

"Ice Palace chocolate is a good incentive to set down roots as any, huh?"

Callie put her plastic spoon down and stared off into the night sky. "Roots. They're very important," she said softly.

Reed knew exactly what she was thinking as she added, "Like I said before, it's no secret that my father had a gambling problem, and we kept being evicted. Many of the people we rented from were wonderful— some of them are here right now. They were generous and patient, but we always knew when it was time to find another place. After a while, no one really wanted to rent to us, but because of the kindness of the Beaumont people who knew that my mother was fighting cancer, and I was trying to get my business going, they continued to help us."

Tears misted her eyes and Reed wished he could have helped her, too.

He'd had no idea. She'd been struggling to keep a roof

over her family's head and he'd been off riding bulls and having a great time. If he'd failed, he'd still have a roof over his head, even though Hurricane Daphne and Big Dan had had other ideas.

"I'll bet you worked hard, Callie."

"I worked two jobs."

"And then you had enough money to buy a house, so you could stay put, huh?"

She smiled. "We don't have to move anymore, Reed. Never."

"Good for you."

She smiled. "And I just love my house. It makes me feel all warm and happy. It's mine, and no one can take it away from me."

They sat in silence for a while, eating their ice cream. Callie seemed lost in thought, probably thinking of what she'd sacrificed to buy a house at a young age. But if anyone could do it, it would be Callie, valedictorian of their graduating class some ten years ago.

Callie finished her ice cream, drank her plastic cup of water, and threw it in the trash can. Reed ate the last bit of his cone.

She checked her watch. "I think I should take you home. It's been a long day and you should put your feet up."

"Good idea." He hated to leave her when they were having a good conversation, but she was right. His knee was throbbing.

They got into Callie's red-pink sun-bleached SUV and she drove to his ranch.

"Are you coming in?" he asked.

"No. I'm pooped."

"I hear you." He pulled the keys to the front door from his pocket. "Will you be here tomorrow?"

"I'll be working."

"See you tomorrow, then. Sweet dreams."

Her green eyes sparkled in the light of the full moon filtering into her car. Her lips were full and ready to be kissed.

He stretched his arm out on the back of the seat. It would take one move to wrap it around Callie and pull her close to him. He wanted to kiss her, but his gut told him that his kiss wouldn't be welcome.

Not yet anyway.

Reed wasn't going to let Callie go this time. She filled the empty space that was ten years of his life. Sure, he loved to ride bulls, but something had been missing. Roots. He loved the ranch, and never realized how much so until he'd almost lost it.

And tangled in those roots was Callie Wainright.

CALLIE'S HEART POUNDED as she drove home. She'd thought Reed was going to kiss her. Would she have let him?

It was a moot point now, but she wondered how she would have reacted.

She just didn't know.

Pulling into the driveway, she paused to look at her house. It was an old, beige Victorian. Callie and her brothers had painted the gingerbread trim in shades of peach, lavender, pink and yellow.

It was a proud old house, and she was proud of it. Standing tall on the corner of Main Street and Elm, there was almost an acre surrounding it.

She and her brothers had become quite good at carpentry, plumbing and painting. She loved to decorate the Victorian and, since she just loved lace, she'd hung lace curtains, positioned lace doilies and covered tables with lace tablecloths.

Unlike Callie and her mother, her brothers weren't that thrilled with the decor, but they could decorate their rooms however they wanted.

She entered through the side mudroom that led to the cutest retro kitchen that could grace the pages of any magazine.

Callie found her brothers and mother sitting in the living room, talking. She liked the times when they had lively conversations. But when she entered, the room became silent.

"What's up?" she asked. "Did I interrupt something?"

"We were talking about you, Callie," her mother said. "We should have waited for you, so you wouldn't think we were talking behind your back, but your brothers are worried about you."

"Why?"

Her mother smiled thinly. "Because they were afraid that Reed was going to hurt you. However, after talking with him, they think that he's okay."

"Joe... John...you talked to Reed? What on earth did you say to him?"

"We told him not to hurt you," Joe said as John nodded. "Or he'll have to answer to us."

"What?" Callie sank into an armchair.

"We didn't tell him about your other serious fiancés who'd hurt you, but he got the message and our warning," John said as Joe nodded.

They gave each other a high-five and Callie wanted to scream. It was strange to have her brothers making sure she was okay, instead of the other way around, but she could take care of herself.

Actually, they weren't taking care of her, they were interfering.

"You know, you both were only seven years old when

Reed and I went out. We dated from about March until August when he left to ride in the PBR."

That was the best time of her life, when they were inseparable and in love. They'd known each other since kindergarten, so that had meant forever in her book.

"Callie? Hey, Callie?" As if from a distance, she heard John's voice.

"Sorry." Blinking, she returned to reality. "I guess I'm kind of tired, but I want you all to remember that I am twenty-eight years old. I don't need the Touchdown Twins or the Homerun Twins or the Three-Point Twins to defend me. And, Mom, please don't worry about me. I can take care of myself."

"Of course, Callie. Of course. It's just that—"

"I know. My past history with men leaves a lot to be desired." She gave her mother a hug and waved to the twins. "Good night, everyone."

She changed into a comfortable nightshirt and flopped into bed. She was tired and she couldn't quiet her thoughts.

Thoughts of Reed Beaumont.

When Callie arrived at the ranch early the next morning, the door was unlocked.

She cautiously went in. "Reed? Reed, it's Callie."

There was no answer, so she assumed he was out doing something around the ranch. She put her travel mug of coffee on a side table in the office and immediately sat on the floor to do more sorting of the piles she'd left yesterday.

After everything was sorted by year and month, she planned to develop more spreadsheets as needed and entering data. She already had headers and columns in mind...

Much to her dismay, she found herself constantly waiting for Reed to come in from outside. She'd been with him most of yesterday, and he was on her mind when she went to sleep last night, and again the first thing this morning.

She thought about how they made love at their favorite spot, on a blanket alongside the Beaumont River in high school. With a copse of trees that hid them from view, it was the perfect, intimate spot.

They were awkward at first, a mess of fumbling fingers and diverted eyes, until they figured out that it was about making love, and not about sex.

Finally, Reed walked past the arched doorway between the office and the kitchen, but he was coming from the direction of the bedrooms, and not from outside.

Callie watched quietly in the archway as he filled a glass coffeepot with water. He was wearing a pair of black sweatpants that hung low on his hips. He was shirtless, and she could see every muscle and scar on his body—scars from bull riding. When he walked, his muscles bunched and relaxed.

He rubbed his chest and gave a major yawn to wash away the sleep. He said one word. "Coffee."

"I'll share my Thermos with you," she said.

He dropped his crutches and they clanged on the stone floor of the kitchen. "What the hell?"

"Reed, it's Callie." She walked into the kitchen. "I let myself in because the door was unlocked. Luke gave me a key, but I didn't need it this morning."

"Callie." He raked his fingers through his hair with his riding arm. She could see the hard muscles and sinew. "Why are you here so early?"

"Early? It's seven in the morning."

Okay, it was early to any other human, but not her.

She would have been here earlier, but she'd made pancakes for the twins and her mother and left them warming in the oven.

She wouldn't have missed this for the world. It was fun to tease Reed when he was half-asleep and disheveled.

"You have coffee?" he asked hopefully.

"Coconut caramel with hazelnut creamer."

"That's not coffee. That's a candy bar!" He rolled his shoulders. More muscles. "I'll make my coffee. Then I'll go for a jog. It'll be ready when I get back."

She watched as he poured scoop after scoop of beans into a coffee filter, which he then set into the drip coffee maker and then added water.

"That's going to be strong coffee." She stated the obvious.

"It's cowboy coffee. If a horseshoe floats on the top, it's perfect."

"Seems like I've heard that before."

She returned to the office and remembered what she'd thought of last night: the first time they'd made love. She really had to stop thinking of Reed in that way. It was their history, but not their future. Not anymore.

She heard him crutch in several minutes later. She was waiting for him to realize that he couldn't jog.

"I can't jog. What was I thinking?" he said, scratching his head. "I'm so not a morning person. It takes a while for my brain to start working. When I was younger, my father didn't want to hear it. The stock had to be fed, the stalls needed to be mucked, and there was always fence that needed fixing. I was always busy and, when I wasn't, Big Dan always had a list of things waiting for me and my brothers to do."

"And I am definitely a morning person. I love mornings. Everything is so fresh and clean. The sun is coming up and another day is shiny and new. It's like a clean slate."

Reed nodded. "The night for me is full of excitement and adventure. The PBR events are mostly at night—at seven or eight o'clock—and I wait all day. I hit the gym then I go to the event center. I wait for the smell of popcorn, wait for the arena to fill, wait for the excitement to build."

"That's how I feel when I'm working with a client, minus the popcorn and minus the arena, but I do get excited. No two jobs are the same."

He snapped his fingers. "Callie, have you had breakfast yet?"

"No, I haven't. I made pancakes for my family, but I don't like pancakes. How about bacon and eggs? I know how to cook now, thanks to *What's in Your Refrigerator?*"

"Absolutely not. I am supposed to make sure that you are off your feet as much as possible. So, get dressed, sit down and put your feet up."

"Shower?"

"Go ahead," Callie said. "By the time you are done, I'll have breakfast ready."

As she opened the refrigerator, she thought about his sparkling eyes and winning smile. The gestures made him appealing, but she realized he had another plan and she'd fallen right into his trap: she was making breakfast for him.

As she pulled out a carton of eggs and a package of bacon, Callie could insist that cooking for Reed wasn't in her job description, though maybe it was. She was assisting Reed due to his injury and at the request of his brother.

Right now, it didn't matter.

She was enjoying cooking for Reed and looking after him.

Callie could imagine that this grand ranch was Reed's and hers, and she was making breakfast for their children. She looked at the eggs. Yes! A half dozen kids, maybe more.

But she'd have to find someone who had the same dream as hers. Someone who wanted to live in Beaumont full-time, not someone who was absent more than he was present.

Callie's father rarely came home, and she remembered how she tried not to get too happy because she knew he'd be leaving again soon.

The tension between her parents was obvious as Melvin and Connie Wainright were trying to negotiate a divorce settlement. Her father had wanted to be with Tish Holcomb, cougar, in Tahiti, more than he wanted to be a father to her and the twins.

She peeled off six strips of bacon and laid them in a large cast-iron pan to fry. Inez had a collection of pots and pans in various sizes. "I don't use that fancy stuff," she'd always say when a commercial for cookware came on.

Callie hummed as she set the table, and she never hummed!

But it was that kind of a day. Opening the windows, the breeze from outside mixed the aroma of coffee with that of the bacon cooking. The curtains fluttered in the breeze.

If she lived here, Callie would change the curtains from cotton to lace. She'd also lighten up the decor; maybe she'd start with a light oak table instead of the dark mahogany.

She was getting a little crazy.

She hurried back to the stove and flipped the bacon. Just then, Reed entered the room.

"Smells delicious. Coffee and bacon and eggs." He rubbed his muscled chest and she noticed how he filled out his shirt that the material of his chambray shirt didn't have one crease mark.

He wore a perfectly faded pair of jeans held up by a brown braided leather belt with a silver belt buckle the size of Rhode Island. His boots were shined to within an inch of their crocodile life.

"Have a seat, Reed. Breakfast is almost ready."

He unfurled a newspaper she'd put on the table earlier, began reading and asked her a question about politics. She was ready to quip, "I don't discuss politics at the table," but then realized she could have a lively, intelligent conversation with him. And that's just what happened. She enjoyed sparring with him, and sometimes she might play devil's advocate, just to get a rise out of him.

Callie poured the dark, rich coffee into thick turquoise pottery mugs and found creamer in the fridge. She was sure she'd need to lighten up her coffee so the proverbial horseshoe would sink.

She set the mugs on the table and went back to the stove. "How do you like your eggs, Reed?"

"Over easy with all the slime cooked."

"Over easy. No slime. Got it!"

She removed the bacon, set it on a folded paper towel to drain and popped four pieces of Italian bread into the toaster. Then she cracked two eggs into the pan.

She put all the items that belonged to Reed on a plate, then she took a couple of slices of toast for herself.

"Thanks so much, Callie." He folded the paper and set it aside. "Are you joining me?"

"I'm going to have toast and some sludge—I mean coffee. Maybe I should have my own that I brought."

"And miss genuine cowboy coffee?"

She took a seat across from him and topped off the coffee with creamer. It turned about one shade lighter.

She took a sip. "Wow!"

"I know." He grinned. "It'll give you lots of energy to finish up that mess in my father's study."

"It'll give me a heart attack."

"Speaking of my father, I should see him," he said.

"You should."

He reluctantly nodded. "I will."

"Beautiful day, isn't it? Just beautiful."

Read tapped his index finger on the table. "We should be out in weather like this, not stuck inside visiting Big Dan, although I would like to see him later."

She focused on the curtains blowing in the breeze. They were almost hypnotic.

"Callie?"

"Hmm?"

"Are you here?"

She chuckled. "Barely. You're right about what a beautiful day this is."

"Let's go somewhere. Do something."

"I...don't...think...so." Oh, how she wanted to go play, too. But she'd never felt like this before. The job always came first. Always.

"What do you have in mind, Reed?"

"A picnic by the river." His blue eyes were warm and inviting. "I remember a certain picnic. We made love for the first time. I was as awkward as a teenager."

"We *were* teenagers, Reed. And making love with you was wonderful." She smiled. "And you're right. It was a day like this."

She remembered again how they'd first made love on a blanket on the bank of the Beaumont River. It was a bright afternoon and the sun had warmed their already heated bodies.

It had been Reed's first time, too, which had made it extra special. He'd said that there was no one else he'd wanted to make love with, no one other than Callie.

They'd dropped their clothes and Callie had been embarrassed. But Reed had given her as much time as she'd needed and soon they'd been clinging to each other.

She could still remember the gentle touch of his callused hands—hands worn from ranch work and riding practice bulls. His kisses had been sweet and then more intense. Soon enough, he was ripping into a square of foil with his teeth, muttering, "I've had a couple of these for a couple of years. Luke gave them to me. I hope they still work."

She'd watched, mesmerized and worried, as he'd unrolled the condom over his hard length.

Then he was sliding into her, inch by inch. "I don't want to hurt you, Callie. Let me know if—"

She'd slanted her index finger across his lips. She remembered feeling pain, but not wanting him to stop.

Soon they'd moved together, riding a wave of passion, until he'd stopped and waited. For what? She didn't know.

Then he'd shuddered and, with three more thrusts, she knew why he'd had waited. Soon, wave after wave of pleasure washed over her. Reed had been a gentle and thoughtful lover, and she could remember every single detail of that afternoon as if it happened this morning.

Even after ten years, thoughts of that afternoon would creep into her mind whenever she saw Reed or at the most unexpected times. Her face would heat and she knew that telltale pink stain on her neck and cheek would appear.

Just like right now.

They graduated in May, and at the end of August, Reed had left for his first PBR event and Callie had felt bereft and chilled without the warmth of his body next to hers. She'd missed talking to him, telling him her hopes and dreams, but carefully avoiding talking about her father's gambling and carousing with other women. Women who, unlike her mother, weren't going through chemo and shedding hair all over the house until Callie had helped her shaved it all off.

Reed had continued the parade of men—the parade that had started with her father—who'd walked into Callie's life but then galloped out.

She'd wanted to go with Reed, but what had either of them known about living on their own? They were only eighteen with no means of support. Reed would have had to steadily win a lot of events to support both of them or would have had to steadily ask his parents for money to support them both. That just wasn't the cowboy way, nor was it Reed's.

And it certainly wasn't Callie Wainright's way!

Chapter Six

It's nice having breakfast with Callie, Reed thought.

"You know, Callie, the smell of bacon and coffee reminds me of breakfasts with my family when I was a kid. My mom loved early mornings with everyone around this old table. I can remember everyone talking at one time, and we hated to leave the fun to do chores before school. Nothing too awful, just feeding and watering the horses. That's about all we had time for before the school bus came. On the weekends, we almost jumped out of our pajamas to get outside, do our chores and then the day was ours."

Callie chuckled. "I used to see you three riding ATVs, dirt bikes, go-karts and horses. You guys rode everything. I was envious. You were having so much fun. I wanted sisters to play with."

"I'm sorry, Callie, that you didn't have any sisters. You had girlfriends though, right? I seem to remember you hanging around with Sally Lock and Gigi O'Brien in school."

"Sally and Gigi were good friends of mine, but it was hard to maintain a friendship outside of school. I tried to arrange for them to come over, but it always seemed that we were either moving or unpacking boxes."

He nodded. "I remember when you told me about

moving around so much. I think it was early in our senior year."

Whenever he'd seen Callie in the school office in grammar school, he'd known that it couldn't be for discipline—not Callie Wainright, the girl who always led the class in grades. Later, in high school, he learned that it was because she was reporting changes of address.

"After a while, we didn't unpack the boxes and just left them in the rooms in which they belonged. If we needed something, it was carefully marked on the side in red. It was a lot easier then constantly packing and unpacking."

"Smart." And it was sad, too.

"Necessary."

She barely ate her toast. "I didn't have many friends because I couldn't invite them over. But, of course, I'd be embarrassed to have anyone see our walls of boxes and a couple of old lumpy couches and one beat-up table with equally beat-up chairs. My father had sold the good stuff."

Reed felt like gathering her into a big hug, but it didn't seem to be the right time.

"I'm sorry, Callie. No kid should have to be that wary and distrustful of their own parent."

"There were a lot of good times with my brothers, though, when they got older. We carved out little alleyways for us to navigate around the house. We called it Wainright City. When they were younger, we'd put a blanket over the boxes, like a tent. We'd sit there forever, playing. I'd read in my tent and did hours of homework inside it."

He smiled. "That sounds like it was fun."

"But all throughout childhood, we'd hope that my father wouldn't take our favorite things to sell. Mom purposely mismarked the boxes. Where it said Shorts and

T-Shirts on the box, it was really my doll that I named Mary and little cars the boys collected and played with."

"You had a harsh childhood, Callie. No doubt about it."

She shrugged off his statement. "Looking back, it was my mom's love that got us through it, but my father really hurt her and our little family. He was never there for Mom when she needed him the most."

Reed laid his fork and knife across his empty plate. He'd led a charmed life compared to Callie's, and all that time, he didn't have a clue that he was enjoying his family's big ranch house, while she never really had a home of her own.

Then he'd walked away from her like her father. Maybe they could have worked it out. They could have done *something*, but instead he felt hurt and disappointed and had reacted like a spoiled brat.

Callie watched the billowing curtains for a moment. "I never had it as rotten as some other kids but, to this day, I never let my guard down unless I completely trust the person. Over the years, my trust radar has needed a tune-up."

"Why's that?"

"Because of the men I've dated." She hesitated. "You don't need to hear about my relationship history."

"If you don't want to tell me, that's okay." But he wished she would. He seemed to have caught her in a talkative mood.

It appeared as if she wasn't going to answer him but then abruptly changed her mind.

"You know, Reed, I shouldn't tell you about my past, but who cares anymore? None of them can hurt me. I'm over the whole mess of them."

Reed drained his coffee and Callie got up to pour more.

"You don't have to tell me if you don't want to, Callie. It's your business—"

"It's okay.

She put the coffeepot back in place. "My last fiancé was Mike McBride. He was the cousin of one of my clients, Bob VanPatten—you know Bob. He was a couple of grades above us."

"I remember him. So what happened with Mike Mc-Bride?"

"He went into the Peace Corps. Now, the Peace Corps is a wonderful organization, but Mike could have warned me that joining the corps was part of his future plans."

"He didn't tell you?"

"He sent me a breakup text from Kennedy airport telling me that he was about to step on the plane for Guyana, South America, I was crushed."

Reed swore under his breath. "He was a coward."

"Oh, there's more. Jack Cummings, a CPA that I met when I was taking a class at community college, left me for Florida and the Coast Guard. Another worthwhile endeavor, but, dammit, so am I. He drove over to my mother's house. I wasn't home at the time, so he left a breakup message for me with her then he hopped on a plane."

"Another coward," Reed said.

"Noah Young was in between. Remember him from home room? He went back to his old girlfriend who was in the symphony in Toronto. He at least told me that he was breaking up with me when he'd had too much to drink after we'd gone to a wedding of one of his frat brothers. Liquid courage, I guess."

"You were better off without them, Callie."

"I know that now."

"And I was the first who'd left you, but I asked you to go with me. But you couldn't go. Your family needed you because your father, um…"

"Left my mother for Tish Holcomb He raised an eyebrow then knocked on the table. "What about your father? Do you hear from him?"

"The last that I heard, he was in Tahiti with Tish. She must still have money, but I'm sure that when it runs out, he'll be back."

"But aren't your parents divorced?"

"They are, but somehow they've remained friends through everything. My mom is a better person than I'll ever be."

"I wouldn't say that." He winked. "You're a pretty great person, Callie. You're hardworking—maybe a little too hardworking—and I like it when you really, really laugh."

"And at least you realized why I had to stay. You might have not liked my reasoning, but at least you understood."

"Nope." His nostrils flared. "I do now. But, dammit, not back then when I was in love with you—and I *really was* in love with you, Callie. Maybe I was scared to leave my family and wanted company on the road. Maybe I wanted a cheerleader for just me and not Luke. Who knows? Maybe both. It was a long time ago."

"It's obviously still bothering both of us. It's not the first time we've talked about it."

"Can we start over, Callie?" He'd like nothing better.

"We've started over already, Reed. We're friends now."

CALLIE GATHERED UP the dishes and put them in the dishwasher, wiped off the table and handed Reed his crutches.

"Time for me to go to work, Reed."

"Callie, just a second."

She sat back down and waited for him to speak.

"What do you seriously think about a class reunion here at the ranch? Do you think we could pull it off?"

"Are you looking for me to do the work?" she asked.

"I hoped we could both work together." His eyes were twinkling and he couldn't sit still in his chair.

He wanted to reconnect with his old friends and classmates. He never saw them, unless they approached him at bull-riding events, but Callie saw them all the time, at least the ones who hadn't moved away from Beaumont.

"If you want a reunion, let's organize a reunion. How many grades do you want to attend?"

Just our graduating class. We'll celebrate ten years. That's—what?—about one hundred and thirty people, plus spouses or a guest. We might as well plan for about two hundred," he said.

"We could do a barbecue and amateur rodeo on the Friday night, but let's have a buffet at Al's place. We could book Al's place on Saturday, Reed. Then we don't have to do a lot of work in getting your arena ready."

"Great! Let's do three days—a long weekend. We can have a picnic with everyone's kids on Sunday. We could play ball and have other games for the kids. Nothing special, just hot dogs and hamburgers, potato and macaroni salad and a chef salad."

"And cotton candy, watermelon and ice cream!" Callie added.

"Nice touch."

"How about if we have it at the town square?" She grinned. "It'll just be like a summer picnic. What could be nicer than that?"

He could think of a couple of things but, yeah, a summer picnic would be nice.

"Hmm…" He rubbed his chin. "How about a dinner-dance after the buffet? I can get the Cowhand Band to play."

"Perfect! We can work on the details after my work-day is done," Callie said. "Later, we can find something to eat in the fridge since you're an expert cook now."

"Food! You're a girl after my heart!"

"I'm not after your heart. I know you're just joking, but I'm not in a place to be anything more than friends with you."

"Callie—"

"I know it's been ten years." She sighed. "But we really don't know each other. Sheesh, we didn't even know each other back then. It was a whirlwind summer. We just had a fling—a summer fling before you left for the PBR."

He shook his head. "I was in love with you, Callie. As much as an eighteen-year-old can, I loved you. And what a time we had, Callie. Yee-haw!"

She laughed, and he laughed along with her. Callie Wainright was way too serious these days, and he was just the one to lighten her mood and keep her laughing.

He was going to try like hell.

LATE THAT AFTERNOON, finally, Callie put a stamp on the last thank-you card for flowers, mass cards and donations upon the death of Valerie Lynn over three years ago. On the monogrammed stationery, she apologized for the delayed responses and signed off as "The Beaumont Family."

She also made a spreadsheet of the donors to various charities—names, addresses and other pertinent information—for the Beaumonts to review.

The phone rang.

"I got it!" yelled Reed.

Now that the thank-you cards were finished, Callie reached for a pile of papers she'd clipped together and marked Household Expenses. Booting up her laptop, she began entering information into yet another spreadsheet program. Items without the information she needed would have to be researched to see if it had been paid or not, and what the withdrawal or deposit was for.

Soon Reed appeared at the arched entryway.

"That was Big Dan on the phone. He wants to see you. He also said that he has jobs for you to do. Something about hiring a cleaning service for his apartment and stocking his place with groceries. It looks like Big Dan is going to be released in a couple of weeks and he doesn't want to bother with the mundane."

"I can do all that." She made a notation on a notepad. "I'll need the keys and the address. What else does he want me to do?"

"I'm not sure what else he has in mind. He wants to meet with us tonight at the rehab place," he said. "There goes our planning for the reunion."

"Your father is more important, Reed. We can talk reunion back and forth in my car."

"I hate to keep bumming rides."

"You can't drive, and getting you around and making sure you stay off your feet as much as possible, is part of my Personable Assistance business, so don't worry about it."

"I hope you're getting paid buckets of money to deal with my family," he said.

"I am, but they're not all that bad."

"Like me?" he asked, widening his eyes.

She grunted. "Yes, Reed. You are not all that bad."

"What a compliment!" He snapped his fingers. "And

we'll have to go out for dinner because it'll be late, won't we?"

"Maybe."

The man had a one-track mind, and that track was his stomach. How did he keep so trim and buff?

She knew the answer to that. He worked at it. She should do more. She told herself that she got a lot of exercise just doing errands, but she was kidding herself.

Maybe she and Reed could exercise together!

No. No way. She was seeing way too much of Reed already, and she was going to do what she could to distance herself.

Then it hit her. Beaumont High School reunions were always well attended. If Reed and she were successful in throwing their ten-year reunion, Noah Young, one of those who'd left her, would probably attend.

His presence would ruin the reunion for her.

"Reed, you know you don't have to come with me to see your father. I'm just going to figure out what he wants me to do."

"I need to visit him. Since you're going, I might as well bum a ride. That is, if you don't mind?"

"No. Not at all." In fact, she liked his company. That was because there was nothing between them.

They were just acquaintances, former schoolmates, and old friends. If she had a bit of sentimentality for Reed, it was because he'd been her first.

Of course that was it. Reed Beaumont was her first, and she'd been his.

"You're awful quiet, Callie. Something wrong?"

"Just thinking. Thinking about the past, about the future, about all the things I need to do right now." She retrieved her notebook from the right side of the big desk and leafed through the pages. She really needed to make a new to-do list. She would after she saw Big Dan.

"Are you thinking about me? Which category do I fit in?"

"Reed, you'll always be a part of my past, but right now you're in my present. As for the future, we'll be together because I'm working here, but soon, it looks like I'll be spending some time at your father's apartment."

"I'll help you."

"No. You can't."

"You don't know my father. He can be a real pain."

"Like father, like son. Right?"

He laughed. "Hell, no!"

She handed him his denim jacket from the closet. She retrieved her hoodie. "It's my job. Some of my clients are a dream to work with. Some are not. I'm familiar with Big Dan, and he's a sweetheart."

"Like father, like son."

It was her turn to laugh. "Okay. If you'd like to visit your father, let's go."

They both slipped into their coats. "Always thinking of someone else, aren't you, Callie?"

"What do you mean by that?"

She knew exactly what he meant, but she wanted to hear it from him. "Tell me, Reed." She closed the door and they made their way to Callie's SUV.

"Not now. Not when we're getting along."

He held the door open for her, and they made their way outside. "Which means that we didn't get along before."

"We did. Until you thought about your family instead of yourself."

She stopped with her hand on the door handle of her car. "My mother had cancer, Reed. And she was all alone."

"That was over a year after I asked you to come with me. You could have flown home when your mother got the diagnosis."

"My brothers needed me. They were young and a handful. Mom couldn't take care of them by herself after my father left. Besides, I needed to help bring in money."

"All of that was still after I asked you to come with me."

"Well, dammit, Reed. *You* could have come home. We could have talked more! You could have called *me*." She opened the door of her SUV, got in and slammed it shut.

He did the same. "*You* could have come to some of the bull ridings. *We* could have dated. *You* could have called *me*."

"We didn't part on the best of circumstances. We were young and dumb."

"Let's not talk about it anymore," he said. "We just succeed in making each other mad."

They drove the rest of the way in silence.

Reed broke the silence when he said, "Big Dan's in room 4009. Fourth floor of the Beaumont Alcohol and Drug Rehabilitation Center."

She nodded but didn't talk. Reed Beaumont pushed all her buttons.

"You know, Callie, it's not as if we resolve anything whenever one of us brings up what happened ten years ago. We just keep rehashing the same old hash, and we get hurt all over again."

Getting out of the car, they walked to the entrance of the rehab center.

"I agree, so let's stop talking about it."

They signed in and went to his father's room. "Dad. Hey, Dad." Reed stuck his head inside the door of the room. "You decent? I have a lady with me."

"Yeah, I'm decent. Come in."

Callie wasn't prepared to see Big Dan Beaumont. The once exuberant and hearty man looked thin and pale. His once booming voice was raspy, as if it pained him to speak.

He stood to shake Reed's hand. He might have still been six foot something, but now he hunched over as if sorrow had an actual weight.

"And this is Callie Wainright? It's been a long time, Callie, but you still look as beautiful as a flower garden." He motioned for them to sit on the small couch.

She smiled. "And you're still a charmer, Mr. Beaumont."

"That's what some of the nurses and the counselors say. So does Matty Matthews."

Reed turned to Callie. "Matty was in the same grade as my brother. The two of them were stars on the high school rodeo team.

"I know him, Reed. Remember, I haven't left Beaumont."

Reed raised an eyebrow. "Yeah, I certainly know that."

"And I know Matty."

"Dad, are you off probation now?"

Big Dan shook his head. "No. I still owe probation more time due to my violations. I admitted that I snuck out of rehab a couple of times and there was a little drinking on my part—just a little. Another arrest for disorderly conduct, maybe two. I'll have to check, but I think I owe them another year."

"You can do that standing on your head, Dad."

"I won't be standing on my head, but *I am* going to the gym. I like the gym down the block. And I'd like Callie to find me a good cook—a really good cook. I need to gain some weight. I look like a scarecrow."

Reed shook his head. "Why don't you move back to the ranch? Your old room is repaired. You'd never know that Hurricane Daphne did anything to the house. Besides, I can cook now that I've learned how to make a meal from the fridge."

"I really am excited to be getting out of here and going back to my apartment. And, Reed, remember that it's not my ranch anymore—it belongs to you boys since you bought it at the tax auction. I don't want to move back there. That's why I got an apartment, far away from the ranch." He lowered his head and Callie could see that his eyes were misty. "There are too many memories of your mother there."

"I wish the ranch comforted you, Dad. I have wonderful memories of every square inch of the place that Mom was in. I know she loved us, loved you."

He nodded. "I know, and I'm working up enough guts to move back there, but until then, I'm keeping my apartment in town."

Reed sat quietly for a while then he shifted on the couch. "Hey, Dad, did you see me on TV yesterday doing a cooking show?"

"I saw you," Big Dan said. "In fact, the whole place gathered around the TV to watch. You weren't bad at all." He turned to Callie, "Speaking of cooking. Callie, I'd like you to stop over at Margie Proctor's place. She's a good cook and, wow, can she bake!"

Big Dan's face brightened and Callie suspected that he had more of an interest in Margie Proctor's company than in her cooking. Or maybe it was a little of both. Margie had been a widow for decades, and she was a nurse at Beaumont Hospital. Callie wondered if they'd connected when Big Dan was there last year. If they were happy in each other's company, then congratulations to them both.

She'd like to experience the inner glow that Big Dan had fleetingly showed. Sure, Callie was happy in Reed's company, but she was wary of getting too involved with him. Her heart was firmly surrounded by the wall she'd built brick by brick.

She told herself again and again that she didn't need a serious relationship to make her life complete. Been there, done that.

In fact, a man always threw her steady, calm life into turmoil.

"I'd be glad to contact Margie for you, and if she agrees to cook for you, we can stock your kitchen together. I'll get an estimate of what she'll charge. You'll also need a housekeeper. I suggest the Cleaning Cousins of Beaumont. I'll contact them for you and get an estimate from them, also. They might want to see your apartment."

Big Dan reached into a coffee mug containing pens and pencils and pulled out a ring of keys. He singled out a key and held it up. "This is the key to my apartment. The place is probably very dusty."

"I'll take care of everything, Mr. Beaumont. Don't worry."

"I won't, Callie, and thank you. Reed, thanks to you, too."

"For what, Dad?"

"For helping Callie. And take care of that knee, will you? Luke can't win everything. It's your turn."

Reed laughed as they shook hands. "Thanks for the vote of confidence, Dad."

Callie had confidence in Reed, too. She hoped that he'd win the World Championship and the Finals, but he couldn't get enough points for the Worlds if he wasn't riding.

Chapter Seven

The next morning Reed jumped in the shower, thinking that everything was falling into place for Callie's new business. When word spread around Beaumont that she was working for Big Dan, more and more people would want to hire her.

Ten years ago, one of the reasons she'd had to stay was because her business was just starting. Soon she'd have even more clients than she could handle.

He thought about Callie a lot. In fact, she was always on his mind.

Like now.

He hurried through his shower, so he could put the coffee on. It was great having coffee with her on the old mahogany table, and he was hoping she'd be there again this morning.

Yesterday they'd talked about everything under the sun, and he'd like to do that all over again this morning. If he had his way, after breakfast they'd both adjourn to Big Dan's office. She'd work on her spreadsheets and he'd make some phone calls to hire a construction company. The house of the ramrod, Juan "Slim" Perez, needed a new roof, a new front porch and some cosmetic work both inside and out.

He also wanted a field cleared so wheat, hay and

Reed sure could ride, but could he beat Luke? And what about Jesse? He was riding a hot streak.

Callie's Personable Assistance was growing, but could she keep her mind on business when Reed was always on her mind?

sorghum could be planted. The Beaumont brothers' recent purchase of more horses, bulls and steers from a rancher who was retiring was draining their resources. They wanted the ranch to be self-sustaining.

Maybe Callie could develop a spreadsheet for all the yield from the fields. If they had an overage, it could always be sold. He was also thinking of hiring more cowboys at least for the summer.

He wondered if the Wainright Twins would like a summer job. He'd have to discuss it with Callie over breakfast.

While he was dressing, he heard a knock on the front door.

"Reed. It's me, Callie."

"Callie. Come in. I'll be right with you." She was early. Didn't that woman ever sleep?

He heard her bustling about the kitchen. She was probably making coffee and getting breakfast started. Then he heard her go to in his father's study.

He finished buttoning his shirt and tucked it in, reached for his crutches and hobbled out to the kitchen. Callie was indeed in his father's study. She was typing on her laptop already.

"Coffee and breakfast?" he asked. "I thought we could talk about the reunion."

"Can't. Busy."

"Callie, you just got here and already you are working?"

She slid a pen behind her ear. "Yes."

"Can I bring you a cup of coffee?"

She pointed to a lime green carafe. "I brought my own. It's not as, um, thick…as yours."

He chuckled. "Your loss." He turned to walk toward the kitchen, but changed his mind. "Breakfast?"

"No, thanks. I already ate."

"Okay." He hid his disappointment in a grin, but he wanted what they had yesterday: a nice conversation. Or was it more like playing house with Callie?

Dammit. He was a tough bull rider. He could take life-altering hits from a two-thousand-pound Brahman bull, and now he was turning into a wimp who wanted to sit around his kitchen table and chitchat.

He grunted and made coffee, turning it on to drip. He walked to the fridge to see what he could make himself for breakfast, but Callie stood in front of it with a coffee cup in her hand.

"Hey," he said. "I was just going to play *What's in Your Refrigerator?*"

"I brought some pancakes for you," she said. "They're probably still warm, but I'll microwave them in some paper towels, and they'll be as good as new. I brought some bacon for you, too." She reached into a bag and took out two packs of aluminum foil.

"Thanks for thinking of me, Callie." He wondered if she thought about him like he thought about her.

Probably not.

Bringing him food was just her way of quickly getting back to work.

Her cell phone rang and she hit the answer button. "Hi, Mom...Oh, um, whatever you'd like...Sure, I'll arrange it... When?...Three weeks?...No, that's plenty of time...I'll expect the boys to help...I'm sure they will. Okay...Bye."

She hung up and held on to the counter.

"Something wrong, Callie?"

"That was my mother. Seems like my brothers want a graduation party now. They didn't want one before."

"And you have to arrange it?"

She nodded. "Mom doesn't have the energy, and the boys are always either working out or practicing football."

He wondered why she never stood up for herself and never said no to anyone. He took that back. She'd said no to him.

He put his hand over hers. "Can I help?"

She shook her head, but didn't remove her hand. "This'll be my graduation present to them. I'll make it fabulous."

Removing her hand, she wrapped the pancakes and put them into the microwave.

"Where would it be, Callie?"

"Al's is probably rented already. Maybe I'll get a tent and have it in my backyard."

The microwave dinged and Callie put the pancakes and bacon on a plate. She found maple syrup in the fridge and brought it all to the table.

He sat down. "Smells great."

Callie picked up her mug. "Can I get you anything else?"

"No. Thank you very much. It's nice that you thought of me and went to all that trouble."

Callie waved a hand in dismissal. "It was no trouble. I had to cook for my family anyway."

"Can you spare the time to talk to me? We can do some reunion planning."

She hesitated then nodded as she sat next to him.

"Callie, if you don't want to help me with the reunion, I'll understand."

"The thought crossed my mind that we could combine the two events into one for the day. Half the town would be invited anyway. We might as well invite the *whole* town. There will be a lot of little graduation parties going on, so we might as well have an open house."

"That'd be a lot of work, Callie. You need to think about it more. It's a big undertaking."

She stared out the window. "And there will be no gifts. I'll suggest that guests bring a donation to the Beaumont Food Bank instead."

A donation to the food bank? Callie had a heart of gold.

"Won't your brothers be ticked that they won't be getting gifts?"

"My brothers aren't like that, and because they got full scholarships, all they'll lack is spending money."

"I could offer them jobs for the summer. I've been meaning to hire more help."

Her green eyes twinkled. "You'd do that?"

"Sure I would."

Callie shrugged her shoulders. "But, Reed, they don't know anything about ranch work."

He laughed. "They'll learn. Besides, my hands'll teach them. Don't worry. I won't have them touch any of the bulls."

"Thanks." She let out a deep breath. "John and Joe will love working outdoors. They were getting bored working at Beaumont Pizza during the summer."

"By the time the Beaumont Ranch is done with them, they'll be buff—even more than they are now. They'll certainly be paid better." Reed nodded.

Callie grinned. "Thanks so much. I really appreciate you giving them a job. Believe me, they'll be thrilled. So will my mother."

"Seems like we've been thanking each other all morning."

She laughed. Reed just loved watching Callie's face

... into a big ol' Oklahoma grin. He'd always thought that she was just too serious, but she was coming around.

"I have to go now, Reed. I have a lot to do today." She stood and turned to leave, but turned back. "I have to meet Mrs. Proctor at your father's apartment this afternoon. Would you like to come?"

"Sure. But will you let me take you out to dinner after you're finished?" Reed asked. "How about it?"

MARGIE PROCTOR WAS as delightful as always, Callie thought as she closed her notebook and grinned at Reed. Not only did Margie agree to cook for Big Dan, she was going to clean for him, too.

She was a jovial woman who'd raised five girls after her husband died from a heart attack. Callie remembered babysitting the Proctor girls, and now they all were beautiful women going about their own lives.

Mrs. Proctor might be just as lonely as Big Dan. Callie knew how she felt. On many occasions, she'd felt lonely in spite of living with the twins and her mother.

Maybe that's why she jumped into relationships with men who weren't good prospects for sticking around. Then again, how could she have known that they'd all abandon her?

She shook off her thoughts and listened to Mrs. Proctor.

"I've always liked Big Dan Beaumont," she said. "I'll help him out until he comes to his senses and moves back to his ranch that he'd worked hard on."

"Thanks, Mrs. Proctor. I agree with you," Reed said. "He needs to move back to the ranch, but instead of happy memories, all he feels is sadness. He misses my mother something fierce."

"The whole town loved Valerie Lynn." Mrs. Proctor

folded her hands. "She was a generous woman. Quite remarkable, and I'm sure that all you boys miss her, too."

"We do." Reed smiled slightly, but Callie could tell that he wished things were different.

Mrs. Proctor agreed on the financial terms and thought the apartment was "just adorable" and that the kitchen was "cuter than cute."

Callie exchanged a clandestine smile with Reed. She didn't know about Reed, but Callie had a feeling that it was Big Dan who Mrs. Proctor thought was adorable and cuter than cute.

She stole a glance at Reed. He looked every bit the bull rider that he was. He wore a long-sleeved shirt and jeans—but more than that, the way he carried himself screamed "cowboy." Even his crutches added to the look.

As Reed and Mrs. Proctor talked, Callie studied him objectively. He was handsome, there was no doubt about that. Muscular and buff, with black hair and a five-o'clock shadow, he'd look almost dangerous, if it wasn't for his sky blue eyes.

Her stomach filled with butterflies. She jumped up from her chair. "Reed and I need to get going now, Mrs. Proctor."

Callie had startled both of them, but she couldn't help herself. She needed a diversion from Reed, but she didn't know what that could be. They were going to be sitting in the front seat of her car together, and they were going out to eat.

Like a date?

No. It was no different from when they'd gone to Poppa Al's. They simply had a fragile friendship. There were things said ten years ago that she didn't want to think about.

Reed stood. "Can we drop you off anywhere, Mrs. Proctor?" Reed asked.

"No, dear. I have my car." She grinned. "Are you going somewhere?"

"Out to eat," Reed stated. "Want to join us?"

"Thanks, anyway," Mrs. Proctor said, slipping into her sweater. "But you two run along. Tell Big Dan that I'll start tomorrow with the cleaning and will start cooking when he gets out of rehab."

Callie had never mentioned rehab, but everyone knew. Small town.

Soon everyone would know that she was "dating" Reed.

But she knew better. And so did he.

Mrs. Proctor went her way and they got into Callie's SUV.

"Where would you like to go for dinner tonight?" Reed asked. "What are you in the mood for?"

"Do you mind if we just pick up a couple of subs and eat them at the park? It's a beautiful night and I don't want to be inside."

"Perfect. Is Beaumont Subs still open?"

She nodded. "Open and thriving."

"Let's do it then."

Britt Fielding was working at Beaumont Subs and was very surprised when they walked in. "Reed Beaumont! Is that you?"

"Haven't seen you in a long time, Britt."

"Hi, Callie. Good to see you, too." Britt looked from Reed to Callie and then back again.

Callie grinned. "In answer to the question that you're too polite to ask, the answer is no. We're not a couple. I'm just working for the Beaumont family for a while."

"Too bad. I mean, I always thought you were perfect

for each other. You know, during senior year you two were an item. And I remember the prom—"

"That was a long time ago," Callie said. "And things happen."

"I sure know that. After Phil and I divorced, I was engaged twice, and never made it to the altar."

"I beat you. I've had three serious relationships and they all left me."

Reed gave her the strangest look. "Uh…um, let's order. What's the special?"

"Jason's Favorite. It's named for my youngest. He won't eat anything else. It's a mixed meat sub with lettuce, tomatoes, peppers and onions and my special dressing."

"I'm going to get that." Callie turned to Reed. "It's delicious."

"Make it two then, Britt," Reed said.

"You got it. For here or to go?"

She felt the warmth of Reed's hand on her back. "To go. We're going to have a picnic outside."

Remembering her first and only other picnic with Reed, her face flamed and she hid it by looking into her purse. "It's on me, Reed."

"Not a chance, Callie."

"No way." Britt shook her head. "It's on me for my old friends and schoolmates. Grab some sodas and napkins, too. I'll throw in some paper plates."

"Oh, Britt…that reminds me. What do you think about a reunion for our year combined with the current graduating class?"

She sliced two rolls and layered cold cuts in the middle of both. "Brilliant idea, Callie."

"Callie, I've been thinking. I've been meaning to discuss it with you." Reed rapped the counter with his fingers. "But what do you think about a bigger event? We can have a Beaumont High reunion for all classes and hold it at the county fairgrounds and have local restaurants catering their specialties. Al can feature his Italian dishes, and you can have your subs. Then there's the Beaumont Bakery and the ice cream shop. The sky's the limit."

"What about entertainment?" Britt asked. "Everyone loves the annual bull riding at your arena, Reed. This year, it can be moved to the fairground."

"And we could have a talent contest for entertainment." Callie was getting excited over the whole event. "A big reunion and graduation party. Oh, instead of graduation at the school gym, we could ask Principal McGraw if he'd have the ceremony at the fairgrounds this year, and we'll try and keep the ticket prices as low as we can."

"I happen to know that the fairgrounds aren't booked that weekend, but we need a committee to work with the administrators at the facility," Britt said. "Who do we have so far?"

Reed pushed his hat back with a thumb. "You're looking at them."

"I'll round up my sister, Betsey, and some of her friends. I can get some mothers and fathers from the current graduating class, and, Callie, we can ask some more from ours."

"You and Al Giacomo can always be in charge of the caterers," Callie said, pulling out her notebook from her purse and jotting down some notes.

This was going to be fun.

After more discussion, Callie and Reed left with their subs and walked across the street to the park benches.

A small band was playing in the gazebo and about three hundred people were listening.

"There's one over there," Callie said, pointing to a free bench.

As they walked to the bench, a crowd gathered around Reed. In between slaps on the back, he was autographing every item imaginable. Callie was glad to see that he still drew the line at signing body parts.

She studied him, balancing himself on crutches, smiling and greeting everyone. He was really a nice guy, a hometown hero and not a snobby athlete at all.

Above all, Callie loved how he singled out and gave the young children a lot of attention. He demonstrated how he rode bulls and had them all laughing.

Callie pulled out her notebook and wrote two words: *mutton busting.* It was a way that the kids could "rodeo" by trying to stay on sheep.

A young boy came to the front of the line. On crutches himself, the boy volunteered that he'd broken his leg by sliding into third base.

"Want to race?" Reed joked. The boy laughed but they did manage to race to the gazebo. Reed let the boy win.

Most of the crowd noticed, and they clapped their hands and cheered as Reed lifted the boy's hand in victory.

Callie's heart melted. He was really an excellent role model for children, and she could tell that they really liked him.

Reed would make an excellent father.

Reed a father?

That came from out of the blue!

Reed waved goodbye to all of his fans and returned to the picnic bench. Face flaming, Callie handed him his soda, a plate, some napkins and his sub.

He took a big bite. "This is good. I didn't realize how hungry I was."

She nodded, glad that he hadn't noticed her pink cheeks. "Me, too. Isn't this nice? I have sustenance and music. What more could I want?"

"Maybe a relationship that worked."

"It wasn't to be. In thinking back, I'm glad now. I can't see myself being married to the three guys who took off as fast as they could, especially the two who didn't have the guts to break up with me to my face."

"You'd be hard to leave," he said.

She raised an eyebrow, but didn't say a word. She didn't have to. He knew what she was thinking: *you left and it wasn't hard for you.*

"Sorry, Callie. It had to be rough on you."

"As you well know."

"Yeah, I know."

Callie was desperate to change the subject.

"It was nice talking to Britt about the reunion," she said. "I just love living in Beaumont. Your ancestors founded a great place with great people."

"Yeah. I know. I love coming back here. I just don't do it enough."

"And I never leave," Callie said. "Your roots go deep, Reed. Mine are as short as the last house we lived in."

"But you love your current house now. Right?"

"I love it! It's mine and as long as I keep up the payments, no one can take it away."

"Good for you. Maybe you'll let me see it sometime."

"Of course."

They ate in relative silence, making small talk and listening to the band. Reed's fans continue to walk over to talk to him or to get something signed.

He continued to give each one his full attention, and thanked them.

And Callie continued to give Reed *her* full attention.

REED SIGNED WHAT he thought was his last autograph. The band had finished for the evening and he was finally able to finish his sub.

Callie was looking up at the sky. It was a perfect night in Beaumont. The stars were brilliant against the black sky, he was able to reacquaint himself with his neighbors and their kids, and he enjoyed Callie's company immensely.

Life was good.

He had to leave in two months—at the end of August—and for once he didn't want to go.

He'd certainly miss Callie and the rest of the town. He'd forgotten how close-knit residents of Beaumont were.

In the PBR, he had his bull-riding friends. They were fairly recent acquaintances. But in Beaumont, he'd grown up with half the town.

Callie was right. His roots did run deep. Did he want to cut those roots and stay with the PBR or put his boots down in Beaumont?

Maybe after he won the World and Finals championships he would quit. He was probably the underdog against Luke. His brother was in good health, not injured and able to get on practice bulls.

Yes. After the five days of the Finals in Vegas, Reed wanted to win everything, and finally get out from Luke's shadow.

But where did that leave him and Callie?

Actually, there was no him and Callie. Maybe he

ought to step up his game, ask her out on a special date, like now.

"Reed, we should hit the road. I need to drop you off and get back home. I'll see you bright and early in the morning."

"Let me take you out for breakfast. We'll go to Tootie McGill's place on the golf course," he said.

"Tootie retired. You'll never guess who runs it now."

"Who?"

"Mr. O'Brien. Remember he taught us social studies in freshman and junior year? He retired from teaching and now runs Tootie McGill's. He kept the name.

"But we can't go. You have an appointment tomorrow at the doctor's, and it's going to be a long drive."

"When will you be picking me up?" he asked.

"Bright and early. How about six thirty?" she asked. "Maybe you won't have to use crutches anymore."

"I forgot I had an appointment tomorrow. Where's it at? Clear Springs?"

"It's my job to keep track of your appointments. And, yes. It's in Clear Springs."

"Boy howdy! It would be great to get rid of these crutches."

"I hate to rain on your parade, but don't get your hopes up, Reed. You only had to use them for a couple of weeks."

"Still, I can't wait to get rid of them."

Chapter Eight

Callie sat next to Reed in the doctor's waiting room. He stretched out his leg in front of him. It was now going on an hour that they'd been sitting there, and his butt was numb.

There were only so many old magazines that he could read.

"Reed Beaumont," said a nurse in a colorfully printed top and pants. He got his crutches and hobbled to the door. "Right this way."

"Can I bring my friend?" he asked, not wanting Callie to sit any longer. He also wanted her to hear his good news.

"Sure."

He motioned to Callie to join him. She hesitated, but followed him to an examination room.

"Okay, Mr. Beaumont," said the nurse with the name tag Penny. "Take your jeans off and get up on the table. I'll be right back to take your vitals."

Reed stole a glance at Callie and her eyes were opened wide. He chuckled as he gripped his big belt buckle and gave it a tug.

Callie grinned. "As much as I'd like to take your vitals, Reed, I'm going to go to the waiting room."

He threw his head back and laughed. He really liked it when Callie joked with him.

"You don't have to leave," he said.

"Uh...yes, I do. This is a private matter between you and your doctor, and perhaps Nurse Penny."

"I'll meet you back in the waiting room."

"Okay, but just answer one question for me," Callie said.

"Shoot."

"Briefs or boxers?"

"You don't remember?" he asked. "Maybe I'm giving myself too much credit." He chuckled. "Boxers, the tight-fitting, knitted kind."

Oh, she remembered all right. She just wanted to know if he'd switched.

"I'm still wearing them—not the same pair—but I'm still wearing boxers."

It was Callie's turn to laugh.

SITTING IN THE waiting room, she pulled another dog-eared magazine from one of the stacks. The *Fit and Healthy* magazine cover caught her eye: it was a picture of Reed riding a bull. The headline read The Most Physically Fit Man in America, Bull Rider Reed Beaumont.

The magazine was a year old. If only they could see him now, on crutches, or how, when he ate, he ate like the meal was his last before the electric chair.

She found the page where the article started and looked at the pictures first. There was a shirtless Reed in a pair of black bike shorts doing pushups, a shirtless Reed in a pair of black bike shorts doing sit-ups, a shirtless Reed in black bike shorts running on the beach. He was hot, hunky and solid—a banquet for the eyes.

The last picture was the same as the cover, but this

time it was a centerfold. He was in full PBR dress with his number, two, on his back. His left arm was up, his right hand tied to the handle of his rope. The bull was in a full jump with all hooves in the air.

Callie's heart starting beating wildly and she thought it was fortunate she was in a doctor's office.

She read the article, which listed his winning riding percentages for the year and related how the Beaumont Big Guns had the first three slots tied up out of fifty riders.

Then the article turned personal. They'd asked Reed why he rode bulls. "I like the life, being on the road. I like the adrenaline rush of going against a bull and being in the company of great riders. There's more, but you get the idea."

They'd saved the best for last when they'd asked him if there was someone in his life. "I haven't had a special lady in my life for a long time."

Callie wondered who he was referring to. Was it someone from Beaumont or a woman he'd met on the road? Maybe it was someone who worked for the PBR.

She'd have to remember to ask him about his "special lady."

Her cell phone rang. It was Reed's agent. "Hi, Rick. Reed is being examined by the doctor now…I don't know if he's going to be off his crutches yet…An autographing at the Shoe and Boot Warehouse tomorrow. Where is it?…In Barton Mills? That's a two-hour drive from Beaumont…Of course I'll get him there…Two o'clock… Hold on, here he is now. And, yes. He still has crutches. Okay. Bye."

"I'm sorry, Reed. More time with the crutches?"

He nodded. "But the good news is the doc says that I'm healing nicely."

"Great. You still have to take it easy and keep your leg up?"

"As much as I can," he said.

"Rick just called. You have an autographing session tomorrow at the Shoe and Boot Warehouse that's over at Barton Mills. Do you feel up to it?"

"Sure. I don't want my fans to forget me. Besides, I'm sure it's already advertised that I'll be there. I need to go. Are you able to drive me?"

"Yes. I'll take my laptop and do my work while you're signing. No sense wasting time," Callie said.

"You could do with a little wasted time. Time for yourself."

Callie pointed to the reception window. "Do you need to make another appointment?"

"Two weeks."

The receptionist was very happy to wait on Reed. Callie put the date and time of Reed's appointment in her engagement book and looked up at the woman.

"Do you mind if I take this magazine? It has an article about Reed."

"Sure. Go ahead."

"Thanks."

Callie opened the door for Reed. As they left the office, she looked back and saw the receptionist ogling Reed's butt. She gave a thumbs-up to Callie.

"Absolutely." Callie nodded.

Outside, Reed was walking double-time with his crutches.

"Where's the fire?" she asked.

"Dammit. I thought I could shake these things."

"But you have to be in good shape in two months when you go back to ride. Calm down and do the autographing sessions that your agent sends you to, and just relax."

"I need to ride practice bulls. I think I'll get some of the hands to cull some easy ones out of the herd so I can get a little training in. I'll wear a brace on my knee."

She tossed the magazine onto the front seat. "Have you lost your mind? You have a torn meniscus from a bull, and you think you can ride? Where are your brains, Reed? You might make it worse."

Again, she was glad she was near a doctor's office because she was sure that her blood pressure was sky high.

They both got into her SUV.

"Aw...hell." He shrugged. "I know you're right, Callie. I've only been using the crutches for a couple of weeks, and the doctor is hoping to avoid surgery, but I wish he'd just do it so I can get back to normal."

She started the SUV. "Normal? Beaumont is named after you. You have a historic house and a heritage that is hard to beat. You ride bulls for a living, and so do your two brothers. More than three-quarters of the town was built by a Beaumont. Tell me, what about you is normal?"

"All right. All right. I get your point."

"No practice bulls?" she asked.

"None."

Callie turned onto the highway that led back to Beaumont. "Hey, what's this?" Reed asked, picking up the magazine.

"I found it in the waiting room. There's a great article about you, and you're even the centerfold."

Reed leafed through the magazine. "Hey, I remember this."

"It's a good article." She gave Reed a little time to read it, and then he finally closed the magazine and put it back on the seat.

"So, who's the special lady in your past? Do I know her?"

He looked out the window. "Nah. You don't know her."

"What happened that you're not with her?"

"It's a long story, but she didn't want life on the road. Roots are important to her."

"I can understand how she felt."

"I thought you would," he said. "Um, Callie…I have some builders coming tomorrow morning. I'd love for you to sit in."

"Me? I don't know much about builders or building."

"I value your opinion."

"Okay. Sure. Do you want me to take notes?"

He shook his head. "No way. Like I said, I just want your opinion."

That was really a compliment and Callie was touched that her judgment was appreciated.

"Thanks for the vote of confidence, Reed. I'll help you in any way I can."

CALLIE HAD A quick mind and proved to be the asset he'd thought she'd be. As a result of comparing estimates, time tables, materials and the like, the next afternoon, they settled on three builders, all from Beaumont.

Three projects, three builders.

She opened her briefcase and got out three separate file folders, named them and placed the estimate in the appropriate one. She added his notes and placed everything in a cherry file cabinet.

"They're right in the front of the top drawer in case you need them."

"Thanks for your help, Callie."

"No problem."

She was beautiful, efficient and had brains. But she also took on way too much. He didn't help when he suggested a reunion. That just gave her extra work. And then he suggested she join the contractors' meeting. Yet more work.

Maybe he just wanted to be around her as much as possible.

He should have suggested a picnic or a meal at a restaurant. Or just an evening at the ranch watching the sunset.

"I'll phone the other contractors in the morning and tell them we hired someone," he said. "But I will keep their numbers handy in case something falls through.

She nodded. "I'll get back to my spreadsheets."

He checked his watch. "I don't want to distract you, but I'm starving."

"You're always starving, and you always distract me." She smiled.

"I'd like pizza from Beaumont Pizza. We could get it delivered."

"Great." she said. "Sounds fine. And I can keep on working. I'm way behind. What do you like on a pizza?"
"Anything but anchovies and fruit. I like traditional pizzas."

"Me, too."

That's one thing they had in common, Reed thought. Their pizza toppings. Oh, and eating. They both liked that.

Finally, after what seemed like an eternity, the doorbell rang, and it was the delivery kid with their pizza and a liter of ginger ale. He tipped the kid heavily, and turned to find Callie with her hand out to take the pizza and soda from him so he could crutch to the kitchen table.

Just as they sat down, the ranch phone rang and Callie answered it.

Callie was on the phone for fifteen minutes or so, arranging for a tour and picnic for several grades, and he felt bad that the pizza was getting cold. He could always put some slices into the oven on a pan or something for her.

"Can I warm up some pizza for you?"

"No. I'm sure it's fine."

He put a slice on a plate, handed it to Callie and poured two glasses of ginger ale. He pushed it over to her.

"Thank you." She took a bite. "The first round of tours starts in two days, Reed. It's the usual, hotdogs and hamburgers cooked by your cowboys and some teachers and a tour and lecture about the history of the ranch. The school will supply the food and folding chairs. You know, it's good that some things never change."

"If they were anything like me when I was young, I just wanted to see the livestock and tolerated the historic tour every two years."

Callie took a sip of ginger ale. "I remember how you had to lead the tour of our class. Everyone tried to trip you up with questions, but you knew all the answers."

"If I didn't, my parents would be disappointed. They loved the history of the ranch, especially my mother, and I hear tell that no one expected her to be so enthusiastic because she married into the Beaumonts. She even led tours for the historical society."

"I remember her doing that. I worked there for a while, and booked tours with your mom. Valerie Lynn was a lovely lady."

"Yes. She was, and I miss her every day of my life. I can identify with my father. It hit him hard. When he turned to booze, I added more bull-riding events so I wouldn't have to come home."

She put her hand over his and he rubbed it with his thumb. He liked feeling the contact with Callie, liked the comfort and warmth. Her eyes were misty.

Callie took another sip of ginger ale. "I never thought of it before, but it had to be hard for you to come home this time."

He shrugged. "I thought it would be, but I was glad to be home. It was as if the old place welcomed me back. It was as if my mom welcomed me here, too."

She blinked back tears. "That's sweet, Reed. Really nice." Callie didn't make any effort to remove her hand. Funny, just a while ago, he was hungry. Now he didn't care if he ate. He just wanted her hand in his.

"Please don't cry, Callie. It's all good. My brothers and I saved the ranch from extinction, Dad's about to be released from rehab, the Beaumont Big Guns are leading the PBR World Standings and there's a beautiful woman who's *not* eating pizza in my kitchen."

"Oh, you're not eating, either. I'm sorry." She took her hand from his.

Darn it.

One tiny tear was left on her cheek and Reed stared at it. Reaching out, he wiped the tear with his index finger. It disappeared.

Callie looked at him and for a moment there was just nothing to say. So Reed closed the distance between them and kissed her lightly. First on her cheek where the tear had been, then on her lips.

Reed was tentative at first, and he sensed Callie's hesitation, but she didn't pull away. She leaned into the kiss and then opened her mouth slightly.

He kissed her again and the years seemed to fade. They had graduated. Callie had given her speech as valedictorian and they'd decided to have a picnic on the bank of the Beaumont River and skip all the parties. Instead, they'd had a party of their own.

Reed kissed her now just as he had on the cool riverbank, with his heart and soul and the longing of a future with her.

He'd tried to forget her for ten long years. Sure, there were some buckle bunnies in between, but they'd known beforehand that he was just out for a good time.

He'd measured every woman against Callie and no one could compare to her. Why hadn't he just returned home and dated her?

He'd thought it would be ridiculous to try after the way they'd parted.

So they'd continued as friends. Stopping for a little conversation when they ran into each other or exchanging a wave.

He laid the palm of his hand against her soft cheek.

"It's been a long time, Callie. A long time."

CALLIE COULDN'T BREATHE, couldn't focus. All kinds of thoughts were whirling in her head.

They had been getting along fabulously, and Callie wondered what she'd done for Reed to kiss her like he had.

She'd purposely treated Reed like a friend because she was tired of working at relationships. They'd had their chance ten years ago and they'd gone their separate ways No more falling in love for her. No way.

She'd vowed that there'd be no touching. No kissing. And certainly not the "biggie."

Now she'd just broken her "no touching and no kissing" rules, but she had no intention of making love with him. She'd keep her third rule for sure.

She tried to be casual, like kissing over pizza happened to her every day.

Reed could really kiss. His soft lips were tentative at first, then more demanding, until she couldn't think of anything but his scent and the softness of his hair, that she didn't remember touching.

So what should she do now? She didn't know what to say.

She was twenty-eight years old and she'd just been turned into a quivering mess by Reed Beaumont.

"I'll reheat the pizza," Reed said. "You haven't touched a bite."

"Nether have you. We've both been a little...busy."

They both laughed and that seemed to erase the tension.

Later, they ate the pizza and talked about upcoming events.

Callie checked her notebook. "You have an autographing tomorrow, and the day after, Beaumont Grammar School's first grade is coming for their barbecue and tour, then grade three, then grade five—the rest are going to the state capital."

"What are grades two and four going to do? The usual?"

"Yup. They are in for a historic tour of downtown Beaumont and the historical society," Callie said.

"Some things never change. That's what we used to do." Reed shook his head. "Nothing like a small town, huh?"

Callie gave two thumbs up. "There's nothing like Beaumont."

"Who's going to do the tours here?" he asked.

"You, of course. Who else would know the history of the ranch?"

"Yeah. I guess it's me by default." Reed snapped his fingers. "Wait a minute. How about Big Dan? It would be a perfect opportunity for my father to immerse himself back into the history of the ranch. Besides, he'd love the kids."

"What a fabulous, fabulous idea."

"Yeah. And it'll give him something to do. He needs to keep busy."

"It's really a great idea, Reed." She liked how he'd thought about his father. "Give him a call and ask him."

It was great that Reed had a relationship with his father, even though it might have been hard for him when Big Dan was drinking. Callie didn't have any contact with her father, which was fine with her.

Until Callie bought her own home. Never would her father cross the threshold of her cute beige house on the corner of Main and Elm. He wasn't welcome.

Speaking of which...

"Reed, I think I should be going home. It'll be a long day tomorrow with a two-hour drive up and back to Barton Mills. Your signing is from noon to two."

Reed nodded. "I have to find the time to clean up here tomorrow for the tour. Nothing is all that bad, maybe a little dusty."

"I can help you clean, but first maybe you could remove your gear bag that's in front of the door over there," she said. "And put all your boots in your bedroom closet, cowboy."

Callie got up from the table. "We sound like an old married couple."

He winked. "We do, don't we?"

Chapter Nine

He didn't want to get up, so Reed lay in his bed for a while thinking about Callie, like he had so many times in the past.

Their kisses blasted his boots off.

He could tell she was holding back, and he couldn't blame her. They needed to get acquainted all over again.

Callie was quite a woman. In spite of moving all over Beaumont and dealing with her father's gambling addiction, her mother's breast cancer, and raising her brothers, she was a woman who could handle anything that life dealt her.

Then again, with the exception of her brothers' football game, they'd always been doing things that revolved around him or his family: autograph appearances, TV tapings, working at the ranch and a doctor's appointment to which she was kind enough to drive him.

He was going to ask Callie what she'd like to do. She only had to name it and they'd do it.

He put some coffee on, took a shower, got dressed and crutched out to the barn. Jace, one of the cowboys, was saddle-breaking a horse in the corral. Leaning against the wooden fence, Reed watched and cheered Jace on, wishing he could be the one to break the horse. He and his brothers loved to do that.

He could have asked one of the hands for a ride, but he wanted Callie's company. He chuckled. He was taking her away from her work, and she'd let him know it.

Reed moved on to the ramrod's house, where the construction workers were putting on a new roof. Later they'd relocate to the inside of the house and do some updating. He stopped and talked to the contractor.

On his way back, he went to the barn, where another construction company was adding a tack room to the barn and fixing some things on the inside.

He thought about Callie and how she'd had great ideas after interviewing the contractors. They'd compared notes, had a discussion, and he'd taken her advice.

Another builder's crew was hard at work on the cowboys' bunkhouse. He decided not to level it but to update that, too. And it needed a new roof. He decided not to walk over there.

So he walked to the house to sit outside, to enjoy the beautiful day and wait for Callie to pick him up.

After a short while in the sun, he saw Callie driving down the long dirt road that led to the house. She passed under the cast-iron arch that read Beaumont Ranch, with a big, fancy *B* on top.

Hurricane Daphne had knocked the sign down, but it was the first thing his brother Luke had put back up when he was here.

Whatever construction crew he liked the best would get the job of putting up a portico that used to be there. Hurricane Daphne had got that, too.

His mother had always liked the portico. She could enter the house without getting wet in bad weather.

Callie stopped, and he put his crutches on the backseat and got in on the front passenger side.

He tweaked his hat to her then took it off. "Hi, Callie. Thanks for the ride and for the company."

"You're welcome. I'll find a quiet corner and do some work. Then the day won't be completely wasted."

Wasted?

Obviously she didn't enjoy his company as much as he enjoyed hers.

Callie was very quiet, so the trip was pretty boring. He wondered if she was thinking of the kiss they'd shared. He looked at her flowered blouse and beige shorts that made her look cool and summery. Her blond hair had various shades of gold and yellow, and it shone in the sun.

Callie had beautiful legs and, he had to admit, he was a leg man.

"Hey, Callie. What's on your mind? You've been awfully quiet."

"I'm sorry. I'm just thinking of all the things I need to do. Your agent called me at home last night. Your brothers need plane tickets and hotel reservations to Tucson, Aspen and Billings. There's a lot of arrangements to be made."

"Yeah? What does Rick have them doing?"

"Same as you. Personal appearances and signing autographs. I also have to update all your websites and put the new information up. I noticed that they all need refreshing and some new pictures."

"That's a lot of work, Callie."

"I can do it."

"I know you can, but you need to have fun, too." He grinned. "How about doing something fun? Whatever you'd like to do, I'd be glad to make it happen. Just ask and you'll receive."

"Oh? I have my own genie in a bottle, but no bottle?"

"Callie, if I could rope the moon for you, I'd do it."

"Isn't that from a movie?" She chuckled. "But what would I do with a moon? And I didn't know you could rope!"

She was back!

"Yeah. I can rope. I'm good at it. I used to rope steers. Luke was the header and I was the heeler."

"That's very interesting. Reed, you're quite a cowboy."

"And I miss bull riding. It's been a month since Cowabunga did his thing on my knee. I want to get back on."

"And you go back to your doctor in two weeks. I think you'll get good news. But, Reed, if you draw Cowabunga again, are you going to pass and put him out?"

"Not this cowboy. I'm going to ride him again, and I can't wait."

"Are you serious?"

"Absolutely serious. I ride whatever comes up in the draw, and Cowabunga is a good bull, a fair bull. There's belly rolls and jumping in the air, but, boy howdy, he can buck and spin. The only thing he doesn't do is pull a knife on me." He laughed. "You have to remember that I had eight before he bucked me off and a ninety-point ride. I won the go-round."

"And you got a torn meniscus."

"It's all part of the job, Callie, and I do consider it a job. It's my income."

"I see that the PBR posts your winnings. You Beaumonts win a lot of money."

"We pool our money, and it's all going into the ranch for now—most of it anyway."

"Good for you guys. I know you guys paid all the zillions of dollars in back taxes. We Beaumonters were worried that someone was going to buy the ranch and throw up condos or something worse. Thank goodness you were one step ahead of the tax auction."

"Yeah. We have Luke's wife, Amber, to thank for that. But as long as there is a Beaumont left, the ranch will stand intact."

"Of course, Reed. It's your heritage, your roots."

"It sure is." Something settled inside him. It was… pride.

He was proud of all the Beaumonts that had gone before him, that had added onto the ranch house and bought more land. They'd bought and sold livestock to make it profitable. His father had, too, before Valerie Lynn died. Reed hoped that Big Dan would get his pride back, and bury his hurt when he got to the ranch and gave tours to the kids.

"Callie, you should have a lot of pride, too. You worked hard to buy your house."

"Oh, I am. But you have a history, and I have a beige house."

"History has to start somewhere. Maybe it'll start with you."

REED COULDN'T BE any sweeter—wanting me to tell him something I'd like to do, Callie thought.

She just liked being with him. She always had. There was something about Reed that drew everyone to him like a magnet, Callie included.

As she pulled up in front of the Shoe and Boot Warehouse, he pushed open the passenger door, slid off the seat and stood. Taking his crutches out of the backseat and closing the door, he waited for her to park so she could walk with him.

She slung her laptop case over her shoulder, got out another briefcase full of items along with her purse.

While Reed was signing autographs and taking photos with his fans, she'd be logging in his family's items for their income tax this year.

The workers at the Shoe and Boot Warehouse were happy to pull out a table for her and to get her a chair. If she positioned it correctly, she could watch Reed.

Also with him were three other men, all dressed like Reed, like cowboys. Reed hailed Callie over and introduced her. One was Canadian, one was Brazilian and one came from Stephenville, Texas.

All great guys that she'd watched on TV. They had stacks of pictures in front of them. She picked up Reed's: he was straining as he rode a white bull. The bull had bucked so high that its back hooves could be seen over Reed's head.

"What's the name of this bull, Reed?" Callie asked.

"I believe that he's White Whale."

Reed automatically took the picture, autographed it and handed it to Callie, not picking his head up.

"Oh, Reed!" Callie blinked her eyes rapidly.

Reed looked up. "I just adore you," she joked and waved the picture in front of her face as if she were warm. "You are just *soo* hot!"

The three bull riders laughed. "Oh, Reed!" they crooned. "You're just so hot."

Grinning, Reed held his hands up, obviously enjoying the joke. "Dudes, you're going to be hearing the same thing when the signing starts."

They talked about their last rides. Callie could tell that Reed definitely missed it. Even though the PBR was off during the summer, she knew that most of the cowboys picked up extra circuits, state fairs or rode practice bulls to keep their riding up to par.

Reed couldn't do any of that.

"See you later, Reed. I'm going to do some work."

As she walked away, she heard the three cowboys talking about her.

"Yee-haw, Reed."

"She's a fine-looking woman."

"What's Callie doing with you, partner?"

She vaguely heard Reed explain that she was a personal assistant working for his family.

"Sure. Tell us another tale."

"If you're not dating Callie, I want her number."

Callie looked at Reed, raising an eyebrow. That made her feel good, but, no, she wasn't interested.

Reed held his hands up. "Stop, boys. Let's concentrate on the autographing."

Just as he said that, the store's workers waved in the line of people who were there to meet them.

She could tell by his big grin Reed liked meeting his fans. But he should be a lot better at answering his fan mail.

Thank goodness for her Personable Assistance business.

When she had a moment, she'd update the brothers' websites, or maybe she'd start over. Sometimes that was the better option. And she needed to meet with the reunion and graduation committees.

She took her notebook out of her briefcase and jotted down some notes about everything that was on her mind. Then she got down to the task at hand.

She looked at the box full of paperwork and other items. It seemed like a lot of their transactions for buying and selling their livestock were handshake deals and receipts, if she could call them that, were for everything imaginable, including a paper coffee cup. Just marvelous. At least the sellers forwarded a medical report on each of the animals. She found some and paper-clipped them together. She didn't find anything secured to the paper cup.

But she'd have to find out what the Beaumonts had paid for the animals, and then what they'd sold.

Callie took a deep breath. This was going to be a challenge, but she liked having the Beaumonts as clients. It was so much more fun than working at the historical society, the drugstore, the real estate office and the bakery.

Truth be told, she liked having Reed as a client, but that's how they were going to remain—personal assistant and client.

Then she thought of his kisses again and it made her stomach flutter. It had fluttered a little when she was dating the three who had left her, so she didn't trust her judgment.

But still, like years before, there was just something about Reed.

She'd just have to figure out what.

REED SAT ON a bench waiting for Callie to get his car from the far end of the parking lot. He'd had a great time at the autographing.

Callie made the day even more perfect. They stole glances at each another throughout the event, particularly when he had an over-the-top fan. But they were few, and most of the time, there was a steady flow of bull-riding and rodeo followers.

But he wanted to get back to the ranch. He wanted to check out the progress of the construction workers and the cowboys. He didn't have his ramrod there, so he'd have to oversee everything. While his house was being repaired, Slim Perez and his family were enjoying a well-deserved vacation to Mexico.

Back in the car, they talked about the signing, the reunion/graduating party and whatnot.

A casual conversation, a lot of laughs and a lot of plans were made for the ranch and for the first graders' grammar school tour tomorrow.

Then Reed thought about how Callie had never given him an answer as to what he could treat her to.

"Oh, I'm still thinking about it. I haven't forgotten, but I can't think of anything just yet, but it's in the back of my mind."

"Good, you keep thinking."

"Absolutely."

"Until then, what if I were to think of a few things? Like a movie, or a concert, maybe a play, or we could do some boot scootin'."

"We'll do some boot scootin' when your torn meniscus is gone, okay?" Callie said, opening the door and getting out onto the brick walkway that led to the front porch of the ranch.

"You can scoot your boots?"

She laughed. "Bet your buckle, I can."

"Woo-ee! You're a girl after my heart." He did some dancing steps with his crutches.

"I'm not after your heart, Reed. I know you were joking, but we should probably set things straight. I'm a loser when it comes to men. Remember? I'm not interested in a relationship with you. Can't we just continue to have fun?"

"Sure, we can have fun, but don't put me in the same category as those other guys, Callie. I wanted you to go with me back then, and I didn't sneak off. And you made it crystal clear that I was a jerk for leaving a prosperous ranch for the unknown."

"Wow, was I wrong. You're doing great."

"Maybe you're wrong about us, too, Callie." He raised his hands, palms up, and shrugged his shoulders. "Do you think?"

"Let's not talk about this now, Reed. I still have a lot of work to do today." She felt like curling into herself like a boiled shrimp and sleeping.

"Okay," he said. "I can take a hint, and I'll back off. The next move is yours, Callie. We've already waited ten years. Let's not wait anymore. We should be together, and you know it."

"I don't know that at all. And if you're waiting for me to come to you, you're going to have a long wait."

"Maybe. Maybe not." He took a deep breath and let it out. "Are you saying that our kisses didn't mean anything to you, Callie?"

"No. They did."

"Well, okay then!"

"Let's forget about yesterday, Reed. Please."

She is one frustrating woman!

He shook his head. "You got it, Callie. It's forgotten."

They exited the car and Reed followed Callie into the house, then into his father's den, and watched her gather up a box with a grunt. He wished like hell he could carry it for her.

"I think it's better that I work from my home," she said.

"Why?" His stomach sank. He didn't want her to leave.

"Because I don't want to hurt you, Reed. I will. You know I will." Her eyes watered. "You remember the other Callie, not this one. This one is older…and wiser."

"This one is scared. This one has been hurt." He took her hand and kissed the back of it. "We'll work through it all, Callie. The only way you'll hurt me is to shut down and not talk. Okay?"

She sniffed. "Okay."

"I don't want you to leave. Not when we're getting to know each other again. And you're not a quitter, Callie."

She smiled. "I'm not. I'm glad you reminded me of that."

Dropping the box, she said, "I'll stay, but you stay away."

"No promises, Callie. I did say you have the next move. I didn't say I'd play fair in getting you there."

For the rest of the day Callie entered data related to the Beaumonts' income and disbursement. About nine o'clock in the evening, she called it quits. Looking at her notebook, she realized that she had big gaps in information yet to fill in.

She was about to leave Reed sleeping on the couch, but he suddenly woke. "Huh?" He rubbed his face. "Are you leaving?"

"Yes. It's been a long day."

"Will you be here tomorrow for the school tour?" he asked. "My dad will be giving the lecture and tour."

"I wouldn't miss it." She smiled. "How's he doing with them?"

"I think that Big Dan is doing great with the tours. By retelling the history of the ranch and his colorful stories, it's helping him realize how much he's been missing and now much he *is* the Beaumont Ranch. That's what I'm hoping for anyway, Callie. Thanks."

He seemed so optimistic, and she hoped that things would start to work out for the Beaumont family.

Time to get back to business, she thought. "By the way, do you need me to do anything tomorrow?"

He motioned for her to take a seat next to him.

"I don't remember how we organized the day and my ramrod is in Mexico, but I can speak to some of the hands. They would have participated."

"Good idea, Reed. Do you have a grill for the hot dogs and hamburgers?"

"I saw one on the side of the barn. The cowboys might have been using it, and it's my guess that it might need to be cleaned."

"I can clean it, Reed."

"You'll do no such thing. I think that cleaning a greasy grill is not one of your personal assistant jobs. I'll do it in the morning."

She raised her index finger into the air. "What about entertainment after everyone eats? I remember listening to some cowboys playing the guitar and singing."

"You'll be happy to know that we have a real cool bunch of singers and pickers. They call themselves the Cowhand Band."

"I love it, but will they sing for the kids?" She raised an eyebrow.

"They've already agreed. They'll do all the grades. It helps them practice."

Callie shook her head. "It takes them away from their work on the ranch. Doesn't it?"

"The kids love it, so it's for a good cause. And the cowboys have to take a break sometimes or they'll burn out. Remember that, Callie. You need to take a break sometime, too."

"I rode in the car all day. That's a break," she said.

"But you were still working. Right?"

"Technically, yes. But being with you and talking and laughing isn't like work."

Reed laughed. "Hey, is that a compliment from you?"

"It is." She waved. "See you tomorrow, Reed."

"See ya."

Callie would have to turn away from a kiss if Reed was so inclined, but she was halfway across the room, and he was still sitting on the couch.

"I'll lock the door," she said.

"Thanks."

Reed still didn't move. The least he could do was give her a kiss on the cheek.

But she'd told him to stay away.

It was good that he was listening to her.

Wasn't it?

CALLIE RODE HOME, singing along to the radio so she wouldn't think about Reed. Finally, she pulled into her driveway, behind an old car—even older than her hers—that she didn't recognize.

When she walked into her kitchen, she heard voices raised in anger. There was only one person who'd come into her house and start a fight.

She slowly walked into the living room and tried to quiet her breath and stop her heart from slamming against her backbone. It couldn't be, but there he was. Very tanned. White hair. Potbelly. A Hawaiian shirt and white loafers.

"Father? What are you doing here?"

Chapter Ten

"Why, hello, Callie. How have you been? It's been a long time, hasn't it?"

"Not long enough, Father," she said. "But what brings you to Beaumont? Did Tish Holcomb run out of money?"

The twins snickered.

Her mother shook her head. "Callie, be nice. I can't tolerate a lot of drama."

"None of us can," Callie said. "So what *does* bring you back to Beaumont?"

"John and Joe's graduation, of course," he said.

John chuckled. "Of course. We just told you about our graduation and scholarships tonight. You thought we still had two years left to go in high school."

"Maybe I was a dab off," he joked, and the boys laughed.

What was going on here?

"Father, where are you staying?" Callie asked.

"You have a very nice house here. Four bedrooms and a guest room. I got a tour from the twins. The guest room would suit me perfectly."

Callie shot her brothers an I-can't-believe-you-did-that look. They booth shrugged their huge shoulders.

"Oh, don't get your hackles up, Callie," he snapped, then smiled one of his charming smiles. "I'm only kidding.

I knew I'd be as wanted here as the chicken pox, so don't worry. I'll be staying at the Beaumont Inn."

"Your father also volunteered to take me to my chemo and radiation treatments, so the boys don't have to, and since you have to work during the day," her mother said, sitting back in her chair.

"That's not necessary, Mom."

"I'm almost done with them, honey."

Was she the only one that minded Melvin Wainright's sudden reappearance in their lives? Callie wondered.

Callie shook her head. "If it doesn't bother you, it shouldn't bother me."

Her father clasped his hands together. "Callie, I hope I'm not interfering. I want to help."

She took a seat. Was she the only one who figured out the obvious? That Tish must have run out of money.

"What brought you from Tahiti to Beaumont?" Callie asked again. There had to be a reason.

"Tish is having surgery. She didn't want to have it in Tahiti because she wanted Doc Bender to do it."

"I hope it's nothing serious, Melvin," her mother stated.

So, she's at Dr. Jacob Bender's, Beaumont's only plastic surgeon. The plot thickens.

"Tish is just having something tucked, tightened or lifted. Nothing serious, and I told her that she always looks great, but that's Tish for you."

Callie didn't miss seeing her mother touch the bottom edge of her wig. This was the second time in ten years that her mother had lost her hair. The wig was hopelessly outdated, but she hadn't wanted to spend the money on a new one, no matter how much Callie had insisted.

"So, Father, you're going back to Tahiti soon?"

"Just as soon as Tish is ready to leave."

Joe leaned forward and played drums with his index fingers on the edge of the coffee table. "And get this, Callie, as a graduation present, Dad is going to take us back to Tahiti with him. Can you believe it?"

"Don't you guys have to get jobs to put some money away for college?" The grins left both their faces. "I wanted to tell you that Reed Beaumont said you could work for him at his ranch."

Her common sense smothered their joy over Tahiti like a wet blanket.

"Callie, you're too serious. Don't you ever have fun?" her father had the nerve to ask.

"Fun? No, I did not have fun when we were being evicted from house after house, or am I the only one who remembers that? Am I the only one who remembers thugs coming to the house looking for you to repay your gambling debts? Am I the only one who remembers getting public assistance? Or how about something so we could have lunches at school? Mom worked nights cleaning the school when she was able, so I was the babysitter. The twins were seven years old when you first left, so I didn't have much fun, did I?"

Her face flamed and she had to get away. Her father wasn't the first one to say that she was too serious. Reed Beaumont had said it a couple of times.

Was everyone in this house crazy or was it just her?

Her brothers had the sense to look uncomfortable. Her mother shifted in her chair. "Callie, we can talk later when your father leaves, but until then, you need to calm down."

Her father stood. "I was just leaving. It was wonderful to see everyone. And, Callie, if you'd ever want to sit down with me and have a talk, just let me know. Call me at the Beaumont Inn."

He grinned and his bright white teeth glistened in the lamplight. Callie thought that Tish must have great dental insurance.

"And Reed Beaumont…huh, Callie?" her father asked. "Now, there's a great catch."

She stiffened. "I am the personal assistant for all the Beaumonts, and nothing more."

"Too bad." He shook his head. "That's too bad."

"Mom, as soon as he leaves, I'd love to have that talk with you."

"Sure, honey."

"Goodbye, Father. Have a nice trip back to Tahiti."

About a half hour later, her mother knocked on her bedroom door.

"Callie?"

"Come in, Mom. Is he gone?"

"He's gone."

"Mom, I just don't understand you. After all that he did to us, how could you entertain him in my house… I mean *our* house."

"No. You meant *your* house, Callie."

"I had to buy it for us, don't you see? He can't come here anymore and plummet us into debt."

"Honey, one thing I've learned about in dealing with breast cancer is that there are some things that you cannot change."

"I know, Mom. But you fight. You don't give up."

"And we fought and we didn't give up throughout the years. Right? And as a result, we turned out to be a close-knit family—you, the twins and me. It's your father who missed out."

"But I missed out, too, didn't I?"

"Yes, you did, Callie. When I was sick, you watched

the twins. You worked hard. You supported us when I couldn't work."

"I should be...glad?"

"Don't you see? It gave you a backbone. You started your own business. You bought a house."

"It was Father who should have been here taking care of the twins, taking care of you."

"Yes. He should have. But he took off. Some men can't handle stress."

"And young girl can?"

"Callie, you're right. You're right about everything. I can't justify what he's done throughout the years, I can only ask you to forgive him and move on."

"Forgive him? I don't know if I can ever do that, Mom. Don't you realize that I could have left with Reed all those years ago if he had been here to take care of you and the boys? I certainly would have kept in touch with you, but I didn't go. I might have had children by now."

There were tears in her mom's eyes and Callie would rather have cut off her arm than make her mother cry.

"Mom... Mom..." Callie wrapped her into a hug and realized just how thin she'd become. "I didn't mean to make you cry. I'm just tired and had a headache when I walked in. I just wasn't prepared to see Father here."

"I know that now, honey." She tucked Callie's hair behind her ear. "Get some rest."

"Are you really going to let him drive you to your last appointments?"

"Why not? It's the least he can do, so you kids can get a break."

"Do you still love him?" Callie asked, holding her breath.

"I don't like him, but I'll always love the man he used to be. He gave me all of you."

She squeezed Callie's hand, but Callie hugged her close.

"I think I can understand that," Callie said.

When Callie yawned, her mother got up from the bed and motioned for Callie to get under the covers. She laid her hand on the side of Callie's face just like she used to when Callie was young. Then she turned off the lights.

"I'm sorry, Mom."

"I'm sorry, Callie."

CALLIE GOT UP at the crack of dawn, and her head felt full of cotton. She put the coffee on and went to take a hot shower. Looking out the window, she saw the sun rising in an explosion of yellow, golds and reds. It'd be a great day for the first graders to experience the history of their town, eat a great lunch that would be cooked by real cowboys. Then they'd be entertained by the Cowhand Band.

It'd be fun being on the other side of the tour.

Callie dressed in her oldest clothes and grabbed a box of rubber gloves along with various cleaning supplies. Then she packed an extra outfit.

After munching on some toast with peanut butter, filling her carafe with coffee, she drove to the Beaumont Ranch.

Callie always enjoyed the ride to the ranch. A fine mist blanketed the fields as well as the cows and horses that were grazing. The sunrise added a surreal glow to the countryside.

She turned right, drove under the Beaumont arch and went straight to the horse barn and parked.

To help Reed, she was going to clean the grill.

It was huge, with two lids and a separate smoker unit. Gingerly, she opened a lid. It was a tragic mess.

She got right to work, but was interrupted by the sound of the uneven stride of boots on the gravel path.

"Callie, what are you doing?" Reed asked.

"I couldn't sleep, so I thought I'd help you out by cleaning the grill. You were right, your cowboys made a mess out of it."

"That's why I'm here. I was going to do it."

She shrugged. "How? By hanging on to crutches?"

"I would have figured it out." He smiled. "This is so nice of you, Callie, sincerely."

"Seems like I have a lot of energy this morning, and I want to do something physical rather than mental."

"You could always muck stalls," he said with a straight face and then laughed.

"This is a morning where I wouldn't mind doing that."

"What's on your mind, Callie? What's bugging you? Your father?"

"My wha—oh, crap!" She stopped scrubbing. "How do you know?"

"Because last night, I saw him at the Cave Bar. He was playing those pull-tab things and scratching out lottery tickets."

"Oh."

"I was having a beer with Buck Delaney. Buck picked me up and we decided to grab a drink somewhere because I didn't have any here. We were talking about our livestock, and I noticed your father—his Hawaiian shirt was hard to miss—but he didn't see me."

Callie kept cleaning with a vengeance. It felt good to use muscles that she hadn't in a long time. She vowed to schedule some gym time into her calendar.

"Okay, Callie, stop." He put his hand on her shoulder. "It's fine. When they fire up the grill, they can burn everything off."

She looked down. Her jeans were splattered, so was her T-shirt, and there was something on her cowboy boots. She brushed it all off.

"Callie, sit with me on that bench over there." He pointed to the front row of dozens of rows of green park benches set up in a half circle. Six royal blue portable toilets were set up on a slight hill and looked like soldiers standing at attention.

Callie couldn't believe that she hadn't seen all that when she'd arrived. But she'd had only one thing on her mind: cleaning the darn grill. Maybe she should have screamed into her pillow instead.

Reed patted the space next to him. "Please sit and relax."

She did and he casually put his arm around her shoulders. Callie didn't protest, but she tried not to lean into him.

"What's going on?" he asked.

"I don't know if I want to think about it."

"But you are thinking about it. No one in their right mind gets up at dawn and says, 'I'm dying to clean a barbecue grill. I wonder where I can find one?'"

She laughed. "I knew where I could find one."

"It's your father, isn't it?"

"He was a big surprise when I came home last night, but what I didn't like was my family making nice to him. Don't they remember how it used to be?"

"You can't forgive and forget?"

She shook her head. "He ruined my life."

"But don't let him ruin your future." He sighed. "Callie, I'm no philosopher or psychiatrist, but that's my opinion. That's my barbecue grill philosophy this morning."

"I like your philosophy." She clasped his hand that

was hanging over her shoulder. "Thanks, Reed. I think everything will be all right."

They sat on the bench for a while, thinking. Then Callie stood. "Do you mind if I change in the house?"

"I ordered a cleaning service. They started with my room, so they're probably done. You can change in my room or wherever else you can find. Mine is down the hall—"

"The last room on the left."

Reed grinned. "Have we ever—"

"No. We haven't. We preferred the riverbank." She grinned. "That was our place. But I've taken the tour, remember?"

Another car drove in, and they waited to see who it was. "It's my dad and his probation officer," Reed said. "That was nice of Matty to drive him over, since Dad's license was revoked. I was going to send one of the hands to pick him up, but Matty was on board already."

"I would imagine that he wants to see how your dad does as a tour guide. And maybe give him some moral support."

"I'll be helping him, too," Reed said.

Soon, Matty drove under the arch with the B on it.

Big Dan got out of the car, and Reed was there to meet him.

Callie loved to see Reed hugging his father. Big Dan had a grin that would outshine the sun,

Callie watched for a while, enjoying the affection between father and son until Reed motioned her over. Reluctant to intrude on such a private moment, she walked slowly while the three men joked and talked.

"Come over here, Callie." Big Dan said, taking her hand. "I always thought that you and Reed were headed to the altar." He held out his hand to her, and as she was ready to shake it, he pulled her into a bear hug.

"I've always liked you." He threw his head back and laughed. "How are you doing as our personal assistant?"

"Mr. Beaumont, I really like being your assistant, but don't expect me to become your daughter-in-law. As for my job, I've been busy, but I love it."

He raised a thick white eyebrow. "What do you like the best?"

"Being here is the best," she blurted. "I love the ranch. I always have. If only the walls could talk, the history they could tell."

"Whoo-ee! If you don't marry her, Reed, I'm going to do it!"

Callie thought how there were shades of the old Big Dan Beaumont present, a larger-than-life cowboy and rancher who fell apart when his beloved wife died in his arms.

"Are you excited to get back to being a tour guide for the kids?" she asked.

"I've been looking forward to it. It'll be just like the old days," Big Dan said.

Callie stole a glance at Reed. That's what he'd wanted, wasn't it? He'd wanted his father to remember the good times at the ranch.

"Do you have a speech prepared, Dad?" Reed asked.

"I could talk about the ranch in my sleep. In fact, I probably have. Don't worry about me." He turned back to Callie. "Now tell me how your mother is doing."

"She's almost done with treatment, Big Dan. Thanks for asking."

"Tell her to come up and have some lunch with the kids and enjoy some entertainment. I'd like to see her and get reacquainted. And what about your father?"

Her mouth went dry. "He's in town for a while before he goes back to Tahiti. He's staying at the Beaumont Inn."

Reed shifted closer to her and slipped his arm around her waist as if to comfort her. She moved away because she didn't want Big Dan to think that Reed and she were a couple.

Matty was strangely quiet and Callie got the impression he wanted to talk to the two Beaumont men alone.

"If you gentlemen will excuse me, I'd like to change, and I have work to do until the kids get here. I'd love to see them."

"Sure," said Reed. "You'll hear the noise of the buses." He checked his watch. "You have a couple of hours yet."

"I'll move my car to the parking lot," she said. "And get it out of the way."

As Callie walked away, she heard Reed say, "Really, Dad. Callie was here before dawn. I found her cleaning the barbecue."

Big Dan answered, "Marry that girl, Reed. She's just like your mother."

REED FELT LIGHTER than he had in a long time. His father was like a new person, a happier person. He had several people to thank for his rehab, especially Luke's new wife, Amber. After she'd arrested Big Dan three times for bar fights, Amber had taken the time to recommend to the sentencing judge that he would be better off in rehab than in jail.

Since he'd been faithfully attending Alcoholics Anonymous meetings, his father was looking better, too. He was looking huskier and he'd lost that sickly white color. Reed had his fingers crossed that the ranch Big Dan had abandoned three years ago would be his salvation.

"How about going to the diner for some breakfast?" Reed asked.

"Let's just have coffee at the house," Big Dan said. "And that's only because Matty—I mean Officer Matthews—and I went to breakfast already."

As they entered the ranch house, Reed watched as his father hesitated. Such sorrow was etched on his father's face. Reed expected some of those lines to vanish when his dad was around the first graders.

He poured the coffee, and they all sat around the kitchen table talking about the day's upcoming events.

Soon Callie came into the kitchen. She wore dark jeans, red cowboy boots and a pastel-colored, long-sleeved shirt. Her hair curled under but her bangs blew upward in the breeze as she walked. She had gold chain earrings that skimmed her shoulders. She looked hot.

"Big Dan, I'm going to get to work in your office. I have a lot of entries to make on my shiny new spreadsheets. So, excuse me. Matty, Reed, I'll talk to you both later."

"Sure," said Big Dan. "Spreadsheets...what the hell?" Big Dan chuckled. "Okay by me."

Reed laughed. "I'll let you know when the kids are here, Callie."

"Thanks, Reed." She turned to leave, but he didn't want her to go.

"Callie, why don't you show my dad your spreadsheets and what you're doing with the receipts and disbursements?"

"Sure!" Her eyes were brilliant with excitement. "I'd love to. I'll be right back."

She brought back a stack of papers about two inches thick. "This is what I've been doing, Big Dan. I've been trying to recreate three years of your livestock sales for your personal taxes. You should have an accountant standing by to correct and refile them. I don't know if you'll get money back or not, but I'll sure try."

Big Dan clapped his hands. "Boy howdy, Callie! You are the best personal assistant I know."

"I'm probably the *only* one you know." She checked her notes. "And I can make a spreadsheet as to vaccinations of your livestock. It'll show what bulls, horses and steers you take to rodeos. I can show their points, their breeding stats—the sky's the limit. There's so many things that I can do to help with the operation of your ranch."

"So, little lady, I shouldn't fight technology. This is the upcoming thing, isn't it?" Big Dan said.

Reed watched as Callie tried not to grin. "It's not the upcoming thing. It's been here for a long time."

"Well, Callie…you keep going, and give yourself an increase in salary—say ten percent. You've done a great job here," Big Dan stated.

That's nice that his father was so generous, and Callie deserved the money, but Big Dan didn't even have a clue if the ranch was making a profit.

Big Dan pointed toward the drive to the ranch. "Here comes the school's refrigerated van with the lunch grub. Time to help them unload. We'll put their coolers down by the cooking area." He nudged Reed's arm. "This isn't my first rodeo."

"Looks like the van knows where to go, Dad. It's not their first rodeo, either." Reed grinned. It was great that his dad remembered. Reed was counting on more good memories.

Two school buses roared down the drive to the ranch house and took the right fork in the road to the barn.

"It's almost show time. Are you ready?"

"I'm looking forward to it. Don't worry about me."

Officer Matthews gave him a thumbs-up. "I'll be going on the tours, if you don't mind, Dan. It's been a long time for me."

"It's been a long time for all of us," Callie said. "Oh, to be back in school! The things that I'd do differently..."

Reed was just about to ask, "Like what?", but he didn't want to put her on the spot in front of everyone. He wondered if she was referring to when he'd asked her to go away with him and if she'd regretted her decision to stay in Beaumont.

Reed had all the roots in the world, and he hadn't stayed full-time at the ranch since he hit the road for the PBR at age eighteen.

And Callie hadn't known a permanent home until she'd bought one.

It's funny how life turns out, he thought. He couldn't change the past, but he could certainly make an attempt to change the present.

If only Callie would meet him halfway.

Chapter Eleven

The kids exited the yellow buses to the shrill of whistles and shouts of instruction from their teachers and chaperones. They lined up and filed into the rows of benches that were set up.

Callie saw Big Dan standing in front of the half circle. He motioned for Reed to join him. Officer Matthews sat in the front row and Callie sat next to Reed.

The teachers called for attention and then Reed introduced his father.

"My father, Dan Beaumont, is the patriarch of the Beaumont family, who settled here in 1889 during the Oklahoma Land Rush. Land and livestock have traditionally been what the Beaumont Ranch is noted for. And now my father will tell you more about our history."

"Tell us about bull riding, Reed," a kid yelled. "You're going to be the next champ."

There was clapping and cheering, and Reed held his hands up. "I'd be glad to, if we have time later."

More cheers.

Reed sat next to Callie.

Callie thought that Big Dan did a nice job with his speech, but a couple times he faltered. Reed got him started again by whispering a couple of words.

Then the tour of the house started. The children were

instructed to keep their hands at their sides at all times. They were perfectly behaved.

One little boy held back and Callie could see the tears forming in his eyes. Reed noticed, too, and was squatting down in front of the child.

"We lost our ranch," he told Reed. "My daddy said that the Beaumonts were too big to compete with. I'm going to miss my animals. My daddy is going to sell them." The tears fell in little rivulets down the boy's cheeks.

Callie turned to Reed and whispered, "Billy is the son of William and Rose Waterson, and the Watersons have a small ranch just on the outside of town, past here. They bought it from Carmen Brady about two years ago."

Callie didn't know that they were losing their ranch, but she knew exactly how the little boy felt.

"You're going to miss your animals, huh?" Reed asked.

Billy nodded. "Uh-huh."

Reed grinned. "Would you like to see mine?"

"Uh-huh."

Reed took Billy's hand. "Come on with us, Callie."

He indicated to the teacher that Billy was going to be with him. They walked to the barn and looked at the horses in the corral.

"They're beauties," Billy said.

"Yep. They are. But, Billy, do you remember Big Dan telling you how this ranch was nothing? It took a lot of blood, sweat and tears and lots and lots of years to get it the way it is." He turned to her, "Right, Callie?"

Callie nodded. "You are absolutely right, but things don't always go as planned. It's not your father's fault, Billy. It's not anyone's fault."

Reed turned to the little boy. "Billy, I'm going to talk

to your father and see if there's anything I can do to help. How's that?"

Butterflies settled in Callie's stomach. Reed couldn't be any sweeter if he tried.

He turned to her and whispered, "Callie, can you help me find out what I can do to assist Billy's family?"

She didn't have to make a note in her notebook; she'd remember what Reed asked, and she'd clear her calendar to help out the Watersons with Reed.

As they stood in line later for hot dogs, Callie couldn't stop thinking about Reed. She knew he was one of the good guys, but to watch him with little Billy... Well, Reed melted her heart.

Then Reed, Callie and little Billy walked over to watch the Cowhand Band. They sat in the front row, and Callie could almost imagine that they were a family. That's what she'd always wanted; that's what she'd probably lost in not marrying Reed when he'd asked her all those years ago.

Reed was about to take Callie's hand, but changed his mind. "This is nice, isn't it, Callie? I hope you're not thinking about work."

"I haven't thought about work in at least five minutes."

"Aren't they great?" He nodded to the quartet.

Reed's good foot was tapping and soon everyone was clapping along.

The quartet started a song about trains and had the kids doing all kinds of train sounds. Reed and Big Dan stood, directing the crowd.

Reed loved a good time, and when she was with him, she was guaranteed one, too.

After that, the kids toured the historic house on their way to their buses and their class trip was over. The singing cowboys and the construction crews went back to work, and so did Callie.

Out the big picture windows, she could see Reed talking to some of the hands. She saw him motion in the direction of the Waterson ranch.

She knew that Reed was going to follow through on his promise to Billy, and Callie wouldn't be surprised if it happened soon.

Callie herself called the county clerk and the tax department. She found that the property was in debt, but not all that much.

She had a little bit of money put away; she'd be glad to help out the Watersons.

When Reed came back in, she told him what she'd discovered.

Reed took his checkbook out of his pocket, wrote out a check for the back taxes and another one to get the mortgage up-to-date. While he was writing, Callie wrote out one for a couple of future mortgage payments.

"Callie? What are—"

"If you can help, I can help out, too," she said.

He grinned. "I'm going to kiss you, you know. Right here, right now."

"Reed… I, um…"

His lips were soft and yet firm. At first, his touch was playful, then he pulled her close, and Callie found herself grasping his shirt and pulling him closer still. She couldn't get enough of Reed, in spite of her resolve to keep her distance.

"Well, what have we here?" Big Dan walked into the room, grinning. Another man was behind him… Her father.

"I think we have a romance going on here, Dan."

"I think you're right, Melvin. We might be in-laws in the future."

Her father looked around the study. "Let's drink on that. I'm buying."

"Father! Don't be ridiculous!" Callie snapped. It was just like him to be that inconsiderate of Big Dan's alcohol problem.

Dan held up his hand. "Callie, I can handle this." He turned to Melvin. "Melvin, my drinking days are over. I've been rediscovering what I'd lost—my boys. Know what I mean? At our age, family is what unites us."

"Is that right?" her father said, turning to Callie. "Someone should tell that to my daughter."

"Father, what are you doing here?"

"Just getting reacquainted with my old friend Dan."

Callie turned to Reed and raised an eyebrow. "Okay, everyone. I need to get back to work. Do you mind leaving the room?"

Her father puffed out his chest. "That's my Callie. She's always so serious."

Callie sat quietly after they left, getting her bearings. Her father's mere presence always upset her. Being here at the Beaumont Ranch with Reed was like a sanctuary, and her father had intruded on that.

Or maybe she was just playing house by being here, imagining that she was the grand lady of the historic home.

No. She was working. And so what if she was? She was just doing her job.

She checked her notebook. There was a meeting of the reunion/graduation committee this evening. She'd work up until the time the meeting started, and would go right from the ranch to Al's, where they were going to meet.

An hour later, as Callie was deep into her work, Reed entered the office.

"Callie, how about dinner with me tonight before the committee meeting?"

"As long as it's not a date."

"Oh, for heaven's sake. Yes. Yes, it's going to be a date. Now, would you like to join me for dinner tonight? How about five o'clock? We'll go wherever you'd like."

"How about the Beaumont Diner? I haven't been there in a while."

"Perfect. I'll be back to pick you up, so to speak."

She checked her watch. Two hours before her "date" with Reed.

She couldn't wait.

"I'M HERE TO pick you up, Callie."

"Already?" Bleary-eyed, she turned away from her laptop, and turned to Reed. "I've forgotten the time. I'm sorry."

He was all spiffed up to go out. His plain white shirt had a creases down the arms so perfect that she could cut herself. His black jeans were tight in all the right places, and his boots, made of some kind of reptile, looked ready to dance the night away. His jet-black hair was still partially wet, as if he just stepped out of the shower.

She needed some time to freshen up, but what she was wearing would have to do. Actually, she was probably overdressed for the diner.

"If you'd like to freshen up, you can use the bathroom in my room," Reed said, but she was already making her way down the hall.

She splashed water on her face in the huge bathroom. It was full of fabulous paintings of the west. Fun paintings. They stopped short of a velvet Elvis or dogs playing poker, but she enjoyed them.

They reflected the fun side of Reed.

She dried her face and looked at herself in the mirror. Her eyes were a little bloodshot, and if she didn't have a meeting tonight, she'd just as soon get some sleep.

She hadn't slept last night, not really.

She put on some makeup and yawned, and yawned until her eyes wouldn't open. She fumbled her way to Reed's bed, fell across it and started to snore.

REED WONDERED WHERE Callie had gone. As far as he knew, she was just going to freshen up and then she'd be ready. Actually, Callie was a natural beauty who didn't need any makeup.

He waited ten minutes longer and began to worry. He crutched his way to his room and heard a motor running.

No. It was Callie making all that noise. His first love. She was snoring like a racehorse.

She was flopped sideways on his bed. Balancing himself, he pulled her boots off and tried to straighten her. With a couple of grunts, she straightened herself.

He took one of the colorful blankets from a rack and covered her. Then he pushed the hair from her face, bent over and gave her a kiss on the cheek.

"For my sleeping beauty," he said. "Judging by your snoring, it seems like we're not going to have a date, after all."

He'd call the head of the committee to tell her that they wouldn't be able to make it and to send the meeting minutes to them. The event was only a month away, so they had to finalize their part and they needed to arrange it with the principal. They also had to contact some of their former classmates who were out of town. It wouldn't be hard. Callie had a list that she'd kept current and everyone was on a LISTSERV. The school had a list of graduates, too, and they were on a LISTSERV. It would be easy to notify them of the reunion.

In fact, Callie was so efficient, she'd probably sent an email already.

Reed sat in one of his side chairs and watched Callie sleep. There were so many things that crossed his mind when he thought of her. Would they have had kids if they'd run off together?

Were they even ready for children at age eighteen when they were mere kids themselves?

Things had changed now—at least she'd agreed to go on a date with him—but it was hard to date Callie, especially when she was in a deep sleep.

He smiled. What did that say for her being attracted to him?

He had to do something to improve his game!

He read a book while watching her sleep. When her hair fell on her cheek, he brushed it away. He was ever so vigilant until he fell asleep in the chair himself.

"Reed? Reed, are you asleep?"

He heard Callie's voice as if she were far away. His eyes slowly opened. His book about animal husbandry slid to the floor.

"What happened to me?" Callie asked. "Did I fall asleep?"

"We both did."

"I'm sorry, Reed. I've never done that before. Shall we go to the…uh…Beaumont Diner now?"

Reed checked his watch. "I doubt it, Callie. It's past one in the morning."

"And we missed the committee meeting, too?"

"Lucky us."

"I'd better get home," she said.

"Why not stay here for the night?"

Callie sat up. "Because I have two brothers who'd fight you. They can't seem to remember that I'm twenty-eight."

Reed laughed. "I can take them."

"I should go."

"It's up to you, Callie. I can sleep on the couch. You'll just have to turn around and come back here in the morning for work."

"No. My mother might be worried, and it's too late to call her."

She stood to get up, tripped over his book and fell into his arms as he tried to catch her.

They stood together in each other's arms for several heartbeats. Slowly, Callie turned her head up to Reed, and studied his face, letting her index finger trace the lines of his jaw, his cheekbone.

He held his breath, waiting, wondering what Callie was going to do next. She was like a little hummingbird that he didn't want to scare off. He didn't want to move for fear that she might stop.

Her hands splayed against his chest, down his stomach then back again.

"Don't toy with me, Callie. I'm yours if you want me, but you'd better stop now if you're teasing me."

She looked longingly into his blue eyes, now as turbulent as a storm. "It has been a long time, Reed."

"Don't worry about it, Callie."

"I just want you to know," she said. "But it's probably like riding a bike, huh? Once you get it, you'll never forget."

He smiled and lowered her to the bed, taking most of his weight off her.

He grinned. "Anything else you'd like to say?"

"MAKE LOVE TO ME, REED. Just like you did on the riverbank when we were young."

"I will."

He undressed her button by button, and she shrugged out of her blouse. He undid the button on her jeans and she gasped, feeling his warm knuckles on her bare skin.

He pushed up her bra and ran his fingertips over her breasts, teasing her nipples.

"Let me get rid of it, Reed." She shrugged out of the pink lace bra and let it drop to the floor.

She liked the feel of her nipples against his shirt, but she wanted more. Tugging at his buttons, she quickly undid them, along with those on his cuffs, and pushed the shirt off him.

In doing so, she uncovered a masterpiece. Running her fingertips down his hard body, she realized that the eighteen-year-old boy had turned into a man with hard muscle and sinew, a man with needs.

She had needs, too.

They quickly dispensed with the rest of their clothes, and Callie liked the feel of his weight on her.

Their tongues danced; their bodies swayed.

"Callie, wait. I'm sorry. I almost forgot." He pulled open his nightstand.

Watching Reed walk around nude was a treat. He really was quite a hunk, and she felt her blood boiling by just looking at his already thick erection.

He opened a foil condom package with his teeth and rolled it down his hard length. When he was done, he returned to Callie's open arms.

They moved together, kissing, laughing, nibbling, until they were both ready.

"Callie?"

"I want you, Reed."

He entered her slowly, then waited. Moving her hips, she took him deep. Then he started to move. Slowly at first, then fast, faster. She met him thrust for thrust until he abruptly stopped and gritted his teeth.

She realized that he was waiting for her to catch up. She moved her hips faster, and then he joined her, picking up the pace.

And after that, they touched the stars, then fell back to earth together in each other's arms and wondering if they'd ever have a future together.

Chapter Twelve

The sun shone on Callie's face as she slowly awoke, but she couldn't move.

Looking down, she saw an arm across her waist. Looking up, she noticed that the arm was attached to Reed Beaumont.

She moved it away, and Reed awoke. "What—"

The clock on the wall said nine o'clock. "Oh, no! Your father and Matty Matthews are going to be here anytime now for the third graders. I don't want them to see us in here together."

She elbowed Reed. "Get up, for heaven's sake."

He mumbled. She got up, gathered her clothes from the floor and jumped into the shower. She turned it up as hot as she could stand it, then as cold.

Reed and she made love three times last night. Three condoms, three times. She grinned as she remembered their night together. No one fit her better than Reed, not that she had much to compare him to. One of her exes had been saving himself for marriage, one had treated her like a breakable figurine and one had grunted like a mule.

All three beat her to the breakup, even though she'd been going to part ways with them first. Still, it did nothing for her ego, the way they'd dumped her.

She had to wear the same clothes this morning, wrinkled now, from her night of passion with Reed.

Wrapping the towel around her wet hair, she went back into Reed's room. He hadn't moved. With boots in hand, she hurried out into the kitchen, where she quickly made coffee.

She should have put her boots on first and brushed her hair because in walked Big Dan and Officer Matty Matthews.

They took in her appearance.

Big Dan raised a bushy white eyebrow. "Hello, Callie. Is my son up yet?"

"Uh…um, I don't think so because he's usually up making coffee before I get here."

Okay, that wasn't a lie, just a simple statement of fact.

"So you haven't seen him this morning?" Big Dan asked, amusement teasing his lips.

"Uh…well…"

Reed padded into the room wearing a striped terry-cloth bathrobe and a smile that would light up New York City. "Good morning, Dad. Good morning, Matty. Isn't it a glorious day?"

Why didn't he just wear a sign that said I Got Laid Last Night by Callie?

The red heat of embarrassment climbed her neck and landed on her cheeks. How could he be so obnoxious?

He leaned against the kitchen counter and actually whistled some frenzied tune as he made the coffee.

Callie couldn't take any more. She hurried into Reed's bathroom, stuffed her feet into her boots and brushed her hair. She dreaded walking back out to the scrutiny of the three men, so she went into the den, turned the light on and sat at the desk.

Later, Reed appeared with a cup of coffee and handed

it to her. She would have kissed him for the coffee, if she wasn't so mad at him.

"Great night, Callie."

"Um, yes." She fussed with papers on her desk so she wouldn't have to look at him.

"Something wrong?" He moved to try to get her to look at him.

How could he be so inconsiderate of her feelings? How could he embarrass her so?

"Do you think that your father and Matty know that we slept together?" she asked.

He shrugged. "Maybe. Why?"

"Because you embarrassed me, Reed."

He seemed genuinely puzzled. "How did I embarrass you?"

"Acting so happy and chirpy."

"But you made me happy and chirpy."

He didn't get it.

"You are incorrigible!" she whispered between gritted teeth. "Now remove yourself and let me get to work."

"Callie, can we talk?"

"Not the right time."

"When then?" He whistled again. That stupid, tuneless song. "I'll leave, and come back when you're in a better mood."

"Please do."

He finally left the room and she heard him talking with Big Dan and Matty—probably talking about how you just can't please women, no how, no way.

Callie sat and looked out the window. The benches were being tidied for the third graders. Down the road came the white food van. It was early, but it came nonetheless.

Everything was taking place just as it had yesterday.

But she was different. Reed and she had given themselves to each other, free and without holding back. It was a beautiful night and in the wee hours of the morning, they'd clung together and dozed on and off until they made love again.

She didn't have to imagine them together and wonder…

Now she knew.

And even before they'd made love, she'd known she loved him.

She'd always loved Reed Beaumont.

CALLIE DRAINED HER COFFEE. She'd probably drunk a whole pot since breakfast.

Callie couldn't stop thinking about her night with Reed. It was like the years had melted away, but their lovemaking was just as exciting and tender as it had been before. Reed remembered what she liked, and didn't hesitate to use it. He had her swooning.

And she knew exactly what he wanted. Her hands and fingers worked their magic on him, and she loved when he moaned and groaned under her ministrations.

But she really ought to be thinking about her job rather than Reed Beaumont.

She dived into gathering together individual paperwork pertaining to each Beaumont brother and entering whatever she had on their specific spreadsheets. She'd contact their banks and fill in what was missing and what she needed.

She'd saved Reed's for last. Luke's and Jessie's were pretty much straightforward.

But Reed's important papers were stuffed into three huge bubble mailers marked Important Papers.

In spite of being miffed at him, she had to grin.

Shaking out the contents, bank statements and receipts piled onto the desk, Callie saw money orders and investment statements totally hundreds of thousands of dollars. There were several computer printouts, statements from something called JFW Investments and handwritten notes that looked like some kind of stock tips, she guessed.

It was a mishmash of... What?

She read, stared and sorted for over an hour. A pattern began to develop and she sat back in her chair, dumbstruck.

What was Reed doing?

Then the answer came to her loud and clear: he was buying, selling and trading in stocks—a lot.

Callie felt nauseous. No. He couldn't be. It was like gambling to her. He was bandying about extra cash, while she had to work for every penny. She knew it triggered her insecurities about her dad, but she couldn't help it.

There was gambling like her father loved—cards, wheels, slot machines, horses, sports parlays—but whatever Reed was doing was different, but she considered it gambling, absolutely.

She saw one receipt totaling over fifteen thousand dollars. What she could do with that money! She'd pay it on some of the twins' medical bills...or those of her mother's that insurance didn't pay. What a waste! Callie put her head down on the desk. She thought she knew Reed, but this had come out of the blue.

She had to talk to him, find out about this and what other secrets he was keeping.

The third graders were just as cute as the first graders. Their questions were spot-on, and Big Dan was more relaxed than he'd been yesterday.

As Reed listened to the Cowhand Band, he wondered

what Callie was doing. He thought she'd join him for the music and picnic, but she was clearly miffed at his cheerful demeanor this morning.

Thinking of Callie, he grinned. He'd been waiting for her to realize that they belonged together and that they'd wasted too many years.

He loved her.

That's what had really sunk in this morning. That's why he was just so damn happy. He wanted to shout it to the world.

She might have shared his happiness, if she wasn't so embarrassed. He understood how she felt now. He got it.

It had been a long time since he felt like this. Ten years, to be exact. It was lonely on the road, he had to admit. Sure, he had his friends and his fellow riders, but a special person eluded him.

He really should walk up to the big house and apologize to Callie. Checking his watch, he saw that he had a window of opportunity to talk to her.

He took his father aside and told him where he was going. Making the trek up the slight hill, he walked to the patio doors and peeked in. He saw her pouring over a desk full of documents.

"Hi, Callie."

She looked up from her work, a fistful of papers in her hand.

"What's all that?"

"This is your stuff. You tell me."

He noticed that the sparkle had left her eyes and her cheeks were a bright pink.

What happened?

He crutched over to the desk, and glanced at what she'd been doing.

"That's all my investment stuff, huh?" He shrugged. "Is there a problem?"

"Maybe." She sighed. "It's probably none of my business, but can I ask you a question?"

"Sure. And, Callie, my business is your business, so ask away."

"What's all this, Reed? Are you doing online stock gambling?"

He laughed. "I call it an investment. I buy and sell. I play online with stocks in my spare time. You know, day trading. It gives me something to do when I'm waiting for a PBR event to start, or when I'm in a hotel room, bored."

She wanted to cry. "You're gambling with thousands of dollars."

He shrugged. "I am investing in various projects. I'm not gambling."

"Do you make any money doing it? Or shouldn't I ask?"

"I do well." He smiled. "I'm paying for all the remodeling and construction going on right now from my stocks. It's really my play money."

"It's big money," she insisted. "From what I can tell."

"So? Why is this bothering you, Callie?"

"I didn't know you gambled."

"I don't consider it gambling. It's just… I don't know… investing. I don't know why you keep calling it gambling. It's just fun to do."

"Reed, my father is a gambler. My life was ruined by gambling. I *despise* it with a passion and everything that has to do with it."

He looked at her as if she had two heads. "You have to be kidding. Is this a deal breaker between you and me?"

Tears stung her eyes and she turned away. "I don't

know if we had a deal, Reed. Maybe we just had a great night of sex and nothing more."

"Do you really believe that?"

"I don't know what I believe anymore. I'm so confused. I'm going to leave now, maybe go home." She tried not to cry, but the tears fell down her cheeks and onto her blouse. "I need to get away for a while and do something else."

Grabbing her purse, she left the Beaumont Ranch.

"WHAT THE HELL?" Reed mumbled. He felt like he'd been slammed to the dirt and run over by Cowabunga again.

All this drama was because he invested online?

This was the second time that Callie had blown up this morning.

He never remembered her as being so adamant about what she believed.

The phone rang and he answered it. "Moved up? When…?Okay… I'll be there."

His orthopedic surgeon had to change his schedule, so Reed's appointment had been moved up to tomorrow morning. It was an important visit, in that Reed would find out if he had to have an operation or if the meniscus had healed on its own.

It didn't appear that Callie would be thrilled to see him so soon, nut he didn't want to disturb his father, who'd be lecturing grade five tomorrow, and all of his ranch hands were busy cooking or singing.

He racked his brain to find someone that he could bum a ride to and from his doctor's officer, but he drew a blank. Taxi and bus service hadn't reached this far north yet, and it was too far to hitch to the doctor. He just had to pay a visit to Callie and ask her for a ride to his surgeon. Maybe they could talk, too, and iron some things out.

He'd hitchhike over to her house on Elm. It probably wasn't a smart idea, but he was sure someone would pick him up.

He crossed his fingers and looked up at the ceiling. "Please, let me get rid of these crutches, so I can drive," he said to no one. "And let the doc find my knee is okay, so I don't need an operation."

Should he call Callie before he left the house?

He decided not to. She'd only hang up on him. If he showed up in person, she'd have to talk to him, right?

Before he left for Callie's, he looked up his stock accounts. They were all doing great, except for one. But he decided to keep it instead of selling it after looking at its past performance.

He wasn't gambling. He was making good business decisions. He'd have to point that out to Callie.

Leaving a note on the kitchen table, he went out to the main road and stuck his thumb out. It was a bad idea. Just the walk to the main drag tired him out and made his arms sore. But once he was there, he got a ride right away.

The driver knew who Reed was, and that was why he'd stopped. "C'mon in. I'm Bill Waterson. Put your crutches in the backseat."

"You're just the man I've been wanting to talk to," Reed said, getting into the front seat. "I am a personal friend of your son."

Bill shook his hand, "Pleased to finally meet you in person, Reed. Billy hasn't quit talking about you. Where're you going?"

"Into town. Elm Street to be exact, but I don't want you to go out of your way."

"No problem. How often do I pick up a hitchhiker who's a star bull rider?" He laughed. "What do you want to talk to me about?" Bill asked.

"I'd like to buy some hay from you if you have any extra, and then I'd like to talk to you about renting some of your land for a hay lot. If you plant the hay and harvest it, there will be more money for you, of course."

"You—you... Um, yeah...s-sure!" he said.

"We'll talk money and the details later over a couple of cold ones."

"You got it. And thanks, Reed." He held out his hand and they shook. "Thanks for helping me out."

Reed pointed to Callie's house. "Just drop me off here."

"Sure."

"Oh, and, Bill, if you're selling any animals or have any rodeo stock, I'd appreciate it if you'd give me first look."

"Sure...sure...and thanks, Reed. You don't know how much this means—" His voice choked.

Reed put his hand on Bill's shoulder. "I'll be great doing business with you, and getting to know you. And thanks for the ride."

Reed got his crutches and watched as Bill Waterman drove away. Feeling good about their transaction, he wished he felt just as good about facing Callie.

He went over to her front door and rang the bell. When it swung open, he saw Callie's mom.

"Hi, Mrs. Wainright, is Callie at home?"

"Reed, come in." She stepped aside to let him pass. "How did you get here? I don't see a car."

"I hitched. I got a ride from Bill Waterson."

"Oh, I know Bill and his wife. Fine people. They bought the ranch near yours a couple of years ago."

Reed nodded. He didn't want to be rude, but he was in a hurry to talk to Callie. He might have to hitch back.

"Callie apparently has a headache. She's lying down."

"I think I'm the cause of that headache."

"Have a seat, Reed."

"Mrs. Wainright, please tell Callie that I'd just like to talk to her."

"I'll do that. Let me see if she's awake."

Reed waited in the living room for what seemed like an eternity. Maybe Callie wouldn't see him, after all.

Looking around, he liked what he saw. The room was cozy, but not cramped. The decorations were very personal, things that meant things to a family. Sports trophies were on display along with pictures taken around Beaumont: the court house, the high school, Main Street and the before-and-after pictures of Callie's house. There were family pictures of the four of them together, and individual photos.

He studied the before and after images of the house. "What a difference a little paint makes," he mumbled. "And a lot of lace."

He heard voices coming from the rear of the house.

"I'm just tired, Mother, that's all. I have a lot of balls in the air that I'm juggling."

"The man hitchhiked over here to see you. Go and talk to him."

"Okay, Mom."

After a few moments more, Callie walked into the living room.

Reed struggled to stand.

"Don't get up, Reed. Please sit," Callie said as she took a seat on the love seat opposite him. "What's on your mind?"

"Are you feeling okay?"

"Headache. That's all."

"I was wondering if you'd be coming back to work tomorrow."

"I think so. Why?"

"I'm going to need a ride to the doctor's, if you don't mind. They changed my appointment and my dad and the hands will be busy with the kids, and so will my singing cowboys. I have no one to ask but—"

"But me," she finished.

"It doesn't sound right, but…yes. I was hoping that you'd drive me. I'm sorry to have to ask you because of the way we parted, but I had to."

"Yes. I'll drive you, Reed," she said, not meeting his eyes. "What time?"

"I need to be there at nine o'clock, so how about if you pick me up a half hour earlier?"

"Okay. Anything else?"

Oh. He had to remind her. "Don't forget we have a committee meeting tomorrow. It's at Al's again."

"I remember," she said.

"Will you be going?" he asked.

She crossed her arms. "Of course. It was our idea, wasn't it? I'm going to see it through."

"Good.

"Anything else, Reed?"

Boy howdy, he was sure getting the icy treatment.

He put a hand on each knee and leaned forward. "Is there a chance we could talk about my…my…"

"Gambling?"

"My stock investing," he said.

"No." Callie sighed. "You're not investing, Reed. You're not leaving your money alone and letting it work for you. You're playing with it as if you were playing poker."

"Okay, Callie. It's too bad that you can't see my position. I know that your father's gambling problem has tainted your opinion of my investing, but for heaven's sake, all I ask you to do is to keep an open mind."

"I'll try, but just one thing, Reed."

"Sure. What's that?"

"Business and pleasure doesn't mix. From now on, it's strictly business between us." Her usual spring-green eyes became a stormy emerald. "Strictly business."

"What? Last night, wasn't it special?"

"I slept with a client. That's not how I operate my business," she said.

"Oh, c'mon, Callie. I'm not just a client, and you know it. You have to come up with a better excuse than that if you want to stay mad at me."

She held up her hand like a traffic cop. That's all she was going to say. "I'll drive you home now."

In the passenger seat of her SUV, Reed was fuming. Callie just clammed up when he wanted to talk.

He thought he could connect with her, but the investing thing had shut her down.

For heaven's sake. If she usually shut down when something important happened, then it would be a struggle communicating with her.

Actually, they had the same problem ten years ago. When Callie got something in her mind, it was like pushing a mountain to change it.

They drove in silence.

He sighed. "So you're not going to talk to me, huh? Our relationship, such as it is, is done. Over."

"We'll still be friends."

Steam was shooting out of his ears. "I have enough friends, Callie."

She pulled into the long drive to the ranch house and let him off in front of the house.

"Thanks. See you tomorrow," was all he said. He didn't need this kind of aggravation.

Instead of going inside, he crutched behind the ranch house, past Slim's house that was still being remodeled, until he came to the fence that surrounded the corral. He leaned on a railing, and the horses that were out came toward him, nudging his shirt pockets for treats.

"Sorry, boys and girls, I came unprepared. I don't have any carrots or apples right now." Most of the horses left, uninterested in him, but his favorite, a big black gelding, stood in front of him.

"Hello, Onyx." The horse walked closer toward Reed.

"I'm going to ride you, Onyx. When I don't have to use these crutches anymore, that's one of the first things I'm going to do."

It was getting dark. "I'll see you tomorrow, boy."

Reed always felt better when he was around horses, and did his best thinking on the back of one.

And Reed had a lot of thinking to do.

THE NEXT MORNING Callie sat in the waiting room of Reed's orthopedist. She couldn't stop thinking about what he called "investing."

She wasn't going to budge. Lovemaking was great with Reed, but her knight in shining armor had fallen off his bucking bull.

Maybe she was being difficult. Maybe stubborn. But she had deeply negative feelings about gambling.

She knew what Reed had wanted. Another debate on gambling versus investing.

No, thanks.

Finding out that Reed played around with money after making love with him had sent her into a downward spiral from the peak of happiness to the depths of despair.

She thought she'd known him, but things changed. People changed. Reed had changed, and so had she.

Just after his doctor's appointment, she decided that she was going to throw herself into her work. Hopefully, it would keep her busy and she wouldn't have much time to think about Reed or to miss him.

The door opened and Reed walked out. His crutches were gone. He had a big grin and Callie knew how happy he was.

She stood, ready to leave, but suddenly the floor wasn't under her and Reed was swinging her in a circle.

"Yee-haw! Callie, let's go boot scootin'."

She couldn't help but laugh. If anyone could shake her out of her funk, it was Reed.

But he was the one who'd caused it in the first place.

"Put me down!" she said, grinning and he proceeded to lower her into a slide down his hard body.

When her feet were on the ground, she was face-to-face with Reed. Suddenly everyone in the waiting room faded away, and it was just the two of them gazing into each other's eyes, waiting, wondering.

Callie tried to take a step back, but Reed's arms held her tightly to him.

Slowly he bent his head and his mouth came closer to hers. He was about to kiss her and it would be easy to forget everything and enjoy the pleasure of his touch.

Callie tilted her head and kissed Reed. Then darkness slowly washed over her happiness, and she came to her senses. She just couldn't forget that Reed was like her father, and took a step back. "Reed. I can't."

He nodded, then walked out of the waiting room. Callie followed him to the cul-de-sac in front of the medical center where cars were loading and unloading patients.

"Reed, you know that I—"

"Yeah, I know, Callie. You think that I'm a gambler like your father and you can't stand it. But yet you won't talk to me. I didn't fight for you years ago, and I regret it. What can I say to get through to you?"

She remained silent. But what was there to say? They'd said it all.

Reed shifted on his feet. "I think we need time away from each other, Callie. Maybe ten years wasn't enough."

He raised his hand and a taxi that had just unloaded a patient, stopped in front of him.

"I need time to think, too," he said.

Then he was gone and she was alone.

What should she do now?

She drove back to the ranch and back to her spot behind Big Dan's huge desk. Looking out the window, she saw Reed gallop off on a big black horse.

When he got to the road that went past the barns, he picked up speed. In fact, she watched as he raced the horse up a fairly good-size hill. Then he disappeared.

She doubted that his doctor had approved him riding a horse the next day. What was he doing? He was going to hurt himself all over again.

But he rode like the wind, just like he was going to run out of her life. She just knew it, but she didn't know what to do. They were both at a dead end.

How could she get him to understand her point of view?

Chapter Thirteen

For the next month, Callie immersed herself in her work so she didn't have to think about Reed.

On the phone, she spoke with Jesse and Luke and was able to fill in the receipts and sales of various stock. She logged in all the receipts and disbursements of the contractors working on the various projects around the ranch.

In the absence of the ramrod, Callie did the payroll. Reed was everywhere, and she couldn't dodge him. She didn't intend to avoid him, but it seemed that he was avoiding her.

Callie noticed that Reed was still investing in stocks, and that was disappointing. She'd hoped that he'd stop for her, but that was high expectations. He didn't intend to change, and she wasn't going to change her mind.

He was playing with thousands of dollars. What she could do with that. It might even get her out of debt. Then she noticed that a chunk of money was gone from his usual pot. Fifteen thousand dollars, to be exact.

She wanted to know if he'd lost it, but this was his fund, and it had nothing to do with her or her spreadsheets.

Looking out the window, she saw Reed huddled with

Bill Waterson by the corral. No doubt, they were talking hay lots and horses.

Callie looked around, remembering how the office had looked when she'd first seen it—an avalanche of papers. Now, everything had been entered and filed. Fan mail had been answered. More pictures had been ordered, of Luke, Reed and Jesse riding bulls, to give to the fans. She'd even developed a poster featuring the Beaumont Big Guns and ordered a couple thousand copies of it.

"Well, Callie Wainright, how are you doing?"

Big Dan's booming voice echoed around the room. He was alone and not with his probation officer.

"Hi, Big Dan. I was just thinking that my job here is done. Everything is loaded onto your desktop. Would you like to see what I've done?"

He shook his head. "No. I'm sure it's wonderful, but I'm just stopping in to collect some clothes."

"Are you happy with your apartment and how things are going with Mrs. Proctor?" Callie asked.

"It's going fine. Thanks for arranging it."

"It's what you hired me to do, Big Dan."

"And you're the best thing to ever hit this ranch since I lost Valerie Lynn," he said. "And I mean that."

Her cheeks heated. "Thank you so much."

"I have something to ask you, and I don't want you to be offended. You can tell me that it's none of my business, but I've always been direct."

"Sounds serious." She swallowed hard. "You can ask me anything, but it doesn't mean that I'll answer." She smiled, taking the sting out of what she'd just said.

"Fair enough." Big Dan hesitated. "Okay. Okay. What happened between you and my son? He's not himself.

He was so very happy and now he's moping around like he's lost his best friend, and that was you."

"Um, there's something that's creating a brick wall between us."

"You're upset about your father's addiction, aren't you? I can speak to you about that, Callie."

"And so can I." Her father entered the room. He looked serious, unlike his usual devil-may-care self.

Callie's throat suddenly turned dry and she took a sip of coffee. What was going on here? "We know why you're upset with Reed," her father said.

They each took a seat on the chairs in front of her desk.

"We are addicts, Callie," Big Dan said. "You know I'm an alcoholic and you know that your father is a gambling addict. It's unfortunate, but we are both doing something about it."

Her father leaned forward and clasped his hands. "I'm going to Gamblers Anonymous, Callie. It's time. I've talked to Big Dan at great length, and I'm going to change. I've caused you and your mom and the twins a lot of heartache."

"That's great." She encouraged her father. "But isn't this something you should be talking to Mom about? Or maybe your lady friend, Tish?"

"I already have, and I've asked both of them to forgive me. Now I'd like to ask you to forgive me."

"I don't know if I can, Father," she said.

"Your future may be at risk, Callie." Her father gripped the arms of his chair. "It's because of me that your relationship with Reed in in jeopardy. You think that everyone is an addict. Not everyone who takes a drink is an alcoholic. Not everyone who plays the stock market is gambler. Not everyone who plays cards is a gambler."

"I know that, Father."

"Someday, you'll call me Dad, Callie."

"Maybe someday I will."

"Believe me, I'm going to quit and make amends."

"I wish you lots of luck." It would at least give her something to think about, but she wanted to see results first.

"In the meantime, give Reed a break," he said. "Check out what he actually does before you judge him. Think about it."

She nodded. "I already know what he does." But maybe they both were right. *Maybe I just judge Reed too harshly because of my experience with my father. I'm constantly thinking about Reed's penchant for playing with his money, and I don't know what to do.*

REED FINISHED HIS business deal with Bill Waterson, and handed him a twenty-thousand-dollar check as a down payment for future dealings. He knew just by shaking Bill's hand that he'd get a return on his investment.

This way, Bill could hang on for a while longer. Reed and his brothers would give him as much business as they could.

His father was on board, too. Little by little, Big Dan was getting back into some of the workings of the ranch, and that was fine with him and his brothers.

Reed couldn't help but think that because Big Dan was reciting the history of the Beaumont Ranch to the students might serve to remind him of his heritage, of the good times at the ranch.

Instead of feeling sad about Valerie Lynn, maybe he would see her happiness in every part of the ranch: picking flowers, petting the horses, playing with her boys, hanging curtains.

There had been a glow on his mother's face, just like there'd been one on Callie Wainright's. They both loved the ranch. At first, he'd thought Callie's happiness was for being with him, but it was for her work. Why else could she chuck him like she had?

It had been a month since his disagreement with Callie, and Reed decided to move on. He had to. He had the PBR World Finals to conquer along with the year's standings, but personally, he just wanted to beat his older brother.

It wasn't as if he had a competition going with Luke, but if Reed's personal best was better than Luke's, then Reed would be one happy cowboy.

Tomorrow was Friday, and that was Rodeo Day at the Beaumont County Fairgrounds during the graduation/reunion weekend. He and Luke were going to have a friendly bull-riding competition.

After the Saturday night buffet and dance, where he'd volunteered to sell raffle tickets for door prizes, he was going to leave for Nashville, the site of the first PBR event after the summer break. The money they'd made was going to go for new equipment for the playground at the local day care center.

He'd skip the Sunday picnic at the village square. His knee was perfectly fine, and he was back jogging and working out. He even rode some practice bulls from his own pen.

He'd say goodbye to Callie on Saturday night and they'd continue to be friends.

He'd have to settle for that.

Rodeo night at the fairgrounds was a loud and boisterous event, as it had always been. The Cowhand Band was playing and, when they weren't, the speakers around and in the arena spewed a tinny version of classic country songs.

The people of Beaumont boot-scooted on a cement patio on the outside of the arena. At the northern end of the patio was a knocked-together bar where volunteers were stationed; they were ever-vigilant for underage drinkers and either offered them a soda instead or escorted them off the property.

Earlier, he'd discussed making the rodeo a dry event with Big Dan, and his father assured him that he was going to keep himself so darn busy during the rodeo that he wouldn't have time to even think about drinking. Nevertheless, his sponsor was going to be by his side and Matty Matthews would also be attending.

Reed would keep an eye on his father, too, and probably so would most of the town of Beaumont, which was rooting for him. The man didn't have a prayer of slipping up.

Reed had asked his father to be the rodeo announcer, too, and Big Dan beamed. Little by little, Dan was getting back to his old ways.

Slim Gomez was back and had taken over penning the stock. Reed had made some calls and stock contractors were lined up, eager to be called for the Beaumont rodeo. Even the Waterson ranch had several good broncs they were going to contribute.

Reed saw Callie breezing by on numerous occasions. She had a clipboard thick with papers, and on several occasions, she talked to him either in person or by cell phone.

Their contact with each another was business only, and brief and to the point. There were too many details to attend to, to discuss anything at length.

Juniors from the high school who had their licenses,

along with many volunteers from Beaumont Community College, were parking cars in a field, and, as usual, portable toilets of royal blue were lined up in strategic locations like sentries on the lookout for business.

All was ready, and Reed just wanted to sit in the shade by himself for a while and relax before more people came.

When he turned the corner behind the arena and headed for a copse of cedar trees, he saw Callie.

Callie looked like she was getting up to leave. "Don't worry. I won't bite. I just ate a hamburger. I just wanted to take a break from everything. Looks like we had the same idea."

"I should have grabbed some cold drinks." Reed took a seat next to her on the ground.

"I'm not a beer fan, but I could go for a glass of ginger ale. It's my go-to beverage. Beer for you?"

"I don't drink before I ride, but yeah, beer is probably mine."

There was an awkward silence. Funny how things changed. Before, when they were quiet, it didn't seem as uncomfortable as it did now.

"See? We can make small talk and not discuss important things," Reed said.

She nodded. "Let's continue to make small talk, since we're not getting anywhere with the big stuff. Let me try. We're going to have an excellent turnout."

"I know. And after the stock contractors and a couple more big bills, like the toilets and the entertainment, are paid, when the dust settles, I think we'll have a nice chunk to donate to the Beaumont Food Bank."

"Okay, I'm going to get a little sentimental here, so beware. It's fantastic when the whole town pitches in. I just love the people here and I love living in Beaumont, and I don't know how you can stand life on the road."

He shrugged. "Some people travel for their jobs."

"Not for the entire year, they don't. Not like you. You're never home."

"Miss Wainright, were you keeping track of me?"

Callie's signature blush bloomed on her throat and traveled up to her cheeks. "No, I wasn't keeping track. Small town. Besides, it wasn't so long ago when Amber Chapman had to drag one of you home to take care of things at the ranch. Remember?"

"And I'm continuing the work that Luke started. And Jesse will do the same when it's his turn."

"I've always wanted sisters to play with. Instead, I got two brothers who were ten years younger than I was. I was like their mother at times."

"Be careful, Callie, you might be treading on important issues." Reed pulled a blade of tall grass and put the end in his mouth. "You did what you had to do, and you did a great job. You'll see them graduate tomorrow and go off to college with full scholarships."

"I know. And my mother and I are thrilled. They did great."

"You and your mom did great. From what I heard, your brothers received not only scholarships for athletics but also for academics, too." He paused. "You know, sometimes I think about going to college. I did two years online, but I'd like to get a bachelor's in animal husbandry."

"If you ever settled down, you could go to Oklahoma State for that."

"I know, and so could you. You could get that advertising and marketing degree that you've always wanted before life bucked you off."

Callie had that dreamy look on her face and his heart melted. She needed to achieve her dream, and so did he.

She snapped her fingers. "Maybe we can be students together. OSU is only a two-hour drive from here."

"I've driven twenty-four hours straight to get to a bull-riding event. A two-hour ride is nothing."

Their phones rang. They both answered their calls then hung up.

Callie's eyes glistened like she was trying not to cry. "I guess it's time to get back to work. It's been nice *not* talking to you."

He scrambled to his feet. "We'll have to continue our conversation over a couple of bottles of ginger ale."

"Continue our conversation? Oh, you mean about going to college…um, maybe."

He offered her his hand and she was about to take it, but she got up on her own.

What the hell?

"By the way, Reed. You're not going to ride, are you?"

"I sure am!"

Her sad face got even sadder. "Do you think that's wise? You don't want to reinjure yourself."

"A lot of guys ride with a lot worse."

"That doesn't mean that you should," she said.

"Gee, Callie, you sound like you care." They began walking together. He wanted to hold her hand, but he didn't want the rejection that was sure to come. Why couldn't things have stayed the way they were?

Too bad she'd found out about his playing the stock market. She'd just freaked and then shut down.

Finally, it was time for the little kids to show off. Big Dan was announcing the first contestant in the mutton busting. It was little Billy Waterson.

"Hold him around his neck, Billy!" Reed shouted as they approached the back of the arena.

"Go, Billy. Go!" yelled Callie.

He stayed on, his little arms clinging to the neck of the fuzzy sheep. When the horn blew, Billy rolled off.

He pumped his arm for the crowd and got a great applause.

Someone goofed and a good ten sheep got loose from behind the chutes and raced into the arena. It was a funny free-for-all as the kids decided to run after the sheep to round them up.

The sheep won.

After a while, some men came out attempt to get them back behind the chutes. The men were as funny as the kids.

Callie was bent over, laughing, trying to catch her breath as everyone tried to round up the sheep.

"Open the gate!" Reed yelled, his hands cupping at his mouth. "Open the gate!"

Finally someone listened and the sheep filed in.

Everyone began wiping their eyes and the mutton busting resumed. It was almost as funny.

Reed stole a glance at Callie. She was laughing and looked so ecstatic that he didn't want to burst her bubble and tell her that he'd be leaving after the raffle ticket sales.

The way things stood between them, she wouldn't care.

CALLIE TOOK A seat in the arena after Reed left to get ready to ride bulls. She could sense the excitement building in the arena during the bronc busting and the calf roping.

She loved to watch the ladies, dressed in sequins and

sparkles, ride their beautiful horses around the barrels. She found herself holding her breath several times as barrels wobbled. If the barrel fell, it was a ten-second penalty, and basically, the cowgirl was out of the competition.

RayAnne Warren, graduating with her brothers tomorrow, won the barrel racing.

Then it was time for the bull riding. She wondered where Reed was, but she didn't have to look far for him. He was bending over the chute gate and helping other riders pull their bull ropes.

She enjoyed the sight, along with probably every other woman in the arena.

His brothers and some of the other PBR riders had come in for the rodeo and bull riding. They added a significant buzz of excitement to the event.

Suddenly a wave of sadness washed over her and she felt sick. She was going to lose Reed, if she'd ever even had him.

It soon was Reed's turn to ride. The arena announcer, Big Dan, introduced him and then he announced the bull: Cowabunga. Big Dan added that Reed had specifically asked for the bull.

He must be crazy, Callie thought. Riding that bull resulted in his torn meniscus.

What's he doing?

"Reed's a real bull rider. He isn't going to let that bull beat him again," said one of the attendees.

Or is it personal pride?

She knew a lot about personal pride. It was hard to forgive her father for what he'd done to their family. It was even harder to forgive Reed for being like her father.

Especially when she'd fallen in love with Reed again.

Cowabunga blasted out of the chute and Callie held

her breath. Reed was almost pressed flat against him, his riding arm straining. The bull leaped so high in the air, she could see the hooves above Reed's head. Reed doubled over. The bull started spinning, which was always good for points.

Cassie was still holding her breath when Cowabunga changed direction and Reed barely stayed on. The bull launched into his famous belly roll and somehow Reed righted himself.

The buzzer went off. Reed had done it!

Now it was time for him to get off the back of the bull and safely behind the chutes, just as the bull would be trying to do. Cowabunga would be getting fed. Reed would be trying to get away from the bull and awaiting his score.

Reed leaped off and ran. Cowabunga ran in the other direction. Reed was safe, and Callie could breathe again.

His score was ninety-one out of a possible one hundred.

Callie screamed so loudly, she thought she was going to lose her voice.

Now it was time for Luke.

Like a good sport, Reed pulled Luke's bull rope. Jesse was behind the gate, doing something to help. Callie couldn't tell what.

Big Dan spoke. "Luke Beaumont drew Triple Threat, a bull noted for being mean, and he's a spinner, ladies and gentlemen. Luke had better hang on or he'll be tossed clear to Oklahoma City."

Luke stayed on for eighty-seven points.

Jesse rode his bull for eighty-eight points.

None of them took the event. It was won by a cowboy from Missouri, Ross Clarion.

The crowd filed out of the arena and lined up at the food trucks and the various stands offering everything imaginable. It was the alligator bites that had the longest line.

As Callie waited for the pulled pork sandwiches, Reed appeared at her side.

Excitement shot through her. She was so relieved that he was okay and realized how much she still cared for him. She always had.

"I think a pulled pork sandwich sounds good," Reed said.

He'd no sooner got that out before a group of seven girls, giggling and elbowing one another, approached.

"Hey, Reed. Can we get your autograph?"

Three of them were wearing halter tops and Callie knew what was coming next.

"Sure, ladies. What would you like me to sign?"

Someone handed him a white paper plate and he signed his name with flourish.

A girl with pink dreadlocks stared Callie up and down. "Hey, lady, are you his girlfriend?"

Somehow that made Callie seem old. "We're friends."

"So then he's free to date."

"I think he's free to date anyone over twenty. You have to remember that Reed is an old cowboy and you ladies are…what? Thirteen?"

"Hey, we're fourteen," said another with purple and green hair.

"Sorry, my mistake," Callie said, watching Reed sign a straw cowboy hat.

One of the girls approached and handed him a black felt pen. "What would you like me to sign, miss?" Reed asked.

"My stomach." She batted her eyes in an attempt to flirt.

"I don't sign body parts. And you are a minor, too.

No, thanks. Find some paper and come back. I'd be glad to sign it then."

She made a noise with her tongue against her teeth. "Let's go. This dude's a drag."

"Nah, I want an autograph from him. I'll find a paper plate."

"Me, too!"

They all ran off in the direction of another truck. Someone must be handing out paper plates for autographs.

Cassie turned to Reed. "Hey, dude! You're a drag," she teased.

"That's okay. When I see a gaggle of girls like that, I feel pretty old."

"I was just thinking the same thing," she said, suddenly feeling that her dreams of having children weren't going to happen. "Excuse me, Reed. I suddenly don't feel like eating. I'm going to find a quiet place. Maybe I'll even go home. It'll be quiet there, since my mom and my brothers are here."

Reed looked dumbstruck. Just like the time she'd told him that there was no room in her life for another gambler or something like that.

"Goodbye, Reed. See you around."

"Are you sick? Are you going to the graduation tomorrow?"

"Am I feeling sick? Yes, but it's not what you think. And I'll be at the graduation tomorrow."

Walking away, she looked back. Reed was where she'd left him, but now he was flanked by Luke and Jesse, who were talking to him and then hustled him away.

The local TV station had arrived and was covering the event. Undoubtedly, they wanted to talk to the Beaumont Big Guns.

Callie smiled weakly. The publicity would be good for the weekend.

As she walked to her car, she knew she was walking away from Reed once and for all.

Chapter Fourteen

The graduation party/reunion was a great success. Her brothers looked handsome and serious in their caps and gowns as they marched across the makeshift stage at the Beaumont County Fairgrounds.

Callie and her mother clapped the hardest. Even her father looked like a proud parent, though he hadn't been there while the twins were growing up.

Tish Holcomb was sitting next to Callie's father and her face looked like a plastic mask. Maybe when the facelift settled down, she'd look more natural.

Later, Callie had bar duty on the fairgrounds and therefore was able to talk to everyone personally.

After checking IDs, she poured endless pitchers of beer and soda and had a wonderful time.

"Would you like to dance?"

She looked up from pouring a pitcher of ginger ale and saw Reed.

"Um…"

"It's only a dance, Callie. We're not going to solve the world's problems or even ours."

"I'd love to dance," she said. She pulled up the hinged board and exited the bar. "I'll be right back, Juanita."

"Take your time and dance with the handsome cowboy, *chica*."

Reed took Callie's hand and led her to the dance floor. He put his hand around her waist and heard her quick intake of breath.

The music was slow—a twangy, country ballad of drinking, finding love, losing love, driving fast cars and more drinking.

"Callie, I wanted to tell you that I'm leaving tomorrow for Nashville to meet my brothers. I'm ready to ride again in the PBR."

Her heart sank. "You're leaving tomorrow?"

He nodded. "I need to get back to work."

"But what about your work here? All the construction? It isn't finished yet."

"It's almost done, but my father is going to keep an eye on things."

"I see."

She looked into his sky blue eyes. "Actually, I'm finished at the ranch, too. I can work on my laptop at my house."

She was going to regret having to leave the beautiful house and grounds, but her home was fine to work in.

"Are you looking forward to going back, Reed?"

"Yeah. There's nothing for me here at the ranch."

That was meant for her and she got his message loud and clear. Once they might have had something, but not anymore.

"I wish you nothing but the best, Callie. Maybe I'll see you at some of the PBR events."

"Maybe."

His hand was warm on her back and he navigated a quick turn.

"Reed, we have some unfinished business between us," she said.

"Yeah, I know. But you'll never give me a chance to explain my stock trading."

"I wasn't thinking about that, but I was thinking about how you said that you'd do whatever I'd like—all I had to do was name it."

"I remember. Name it."

"Don't play the stocks anymore," she said, gazing into his eyes.

"I meant that we'd do an activity—bowling, bar hopping, the movies, a restaurant—not that."

"If we have any chance together, you have to give it up."

"I'm going to give it up because you refused to understand." He shook his head. "The money I make is mine. I use it to spread around, like manure. It's not my savings account or anything, but just extra money."

"But you could lose."

"I really don't lose. I'm careful." He dipped her and his face was mere inches from hers. "I wish you could understand." He righted her. "I wish things turned out different for us, Callie. You know I have feelings for you. I've *always* had feelings for you."

Her head was spinning and not from the dip. All she could say was, "Me, too, Reed."

"Goodbye, Callie. See you around." He kissed the top of her forehead and moved away from her.

This couldn't be happening. It was too soon. He was leaving too soon.

"Reed, no. Not yet."

But her voice was drowned out by the music and Reed kept on going, out of the building and off to Nashville, and he hadn't even asked her to go with him.

"HERE'S THE OLD mope himself," Jesse said as Reed walked into the lobby of the host hotel for the Nashville PBR event and joined his brothers.

"He looks like an ad for a zombie museum," Luke said.

"Reed, Jesse's right. You're not yourself." Luke gripped his shoulder. "You have to get your head right, or don't bother riding, dude. You're going to get hurt again."

"I know. I know."

"So why isn't Callie Wainright with you?" Luke asked.

"It's complicated."

"That's a cop-out. Uncomplicate it," Jesse said.

"She thinks I'm a gambler like her father."

Luke rubbed his forehead. "Did you tell her that you're not like her father? That you just play the stocks like a gamer?"

"Several times, but she doesn't get it. Her father is a compulsive gambler, and she's had it rough through the years."

"That's a tough one," Jesse said.

"Why didn't you just volunteer to quit?" Jesse asked.

"I don't know. Just being stubborn, I guess. She shut down, so I guess I did, too."

"And how far did that get you?" Luke asked.

"As far as this hotel lobby," Reed admitted. "And in the company of my ugly brothers."

"I've got company," Jesse said. "She's in my room."

"And Amber is waiting for me back in ours."

"Guess I'm all alone, huh?" Reed shook his head.

"Call her," Luke said. "Invite her to the next PBR event."

"Yeah," Jesse said. "And show her a good time. Maybe you can have a good talk with her."

"We'll talk to her, too. We'll tell her all your good points," Luke said.

"Yeah. That should take all of five seconds," Jesse joked.

"Good night. Say hi to Amber, Luke, and a big hello to your special lady, Jesse. Anyone I know?"

Jesse grinned. "Who?"

"Whomever is keeping your bed warm," Reed said.

"I doubt that you know her."

Luke cleared his throat. "What Jesse is trying to say, Reed, is that Jesse, the party cowboy, doesn't really know her yet, either."

Reed chuckled. "Someday Jesse will find the right lady."

"But it sure is fun looking!" Jesse laughed. "How about it, Reed? Did you find the right lady?"

"I think I did, little brother. I think I did."

"Then go get her!" Luke said.

"Right after I win the event."

"Win the event?" Jesse laughed. "In your dreams, Reed."

"When bulls fly, bro," Luke added.

And they flew.

A FEW WEEKS LATER, they were watching the bull riding in Nashville from Callie's living room.

"He did it! Reed won!" Callie jumped up from the love seat in her living room, clapping and high-fiving her brothers. "Yes!"

"For someone who doesn't care about him, you sure care," John said.

"No kidding," said Joe.

Her mother put her hands up. "Leave Callie alone, boys."

Her two brothers excused themselves and headed for bed. Callie was going to do the same until her mother said, "Let's talk, sweetie."

"Sure, Mom. What's up?"

"I don't know how to begin to say this, but I like Reed, and I know you like him."

Callie leaned forward. "I think I love him, Mom. I think I always have."

"What's stopping you from being with him?" Her mother walked over to the love seat and held Callie's hand.

"I think he has a money problem, Mom. He's too careless with it, I think."

"Is it a problem or is it something that he just enjoys doing?"

"What's the difference?"

"A real gambler won't stop. The mortgage isn't paid and the pantry is empty because he's gambled away every last time. Like your father. Reed might just like the challenge of the stock market."

"Mom, do you think I made a mistake?"

She patted Callie's hand. "Go and talk to him."

"I think he's been trying to tell me that he likes the challenge of the stock market. He calls it his play money."

"Then go, sweetie. Go rope your cowboy!"

"I don't know—"

Her phone rang and Callie didn't recognize the number. "Hello? This is Callie Wainright."

"Callie, it's Bill Waterson. I've been trying to contact Reed Beaumont. Do you think I could borrow a tractor to plant the hay for Reed? Mine bit the dust."

"Hay for Reed?"

"Yeah, we have an agreement that I'd plant a hay lot for the Beaumont stock on my land. Reed's paying me."

"Oh, I understand now, Mr. Waterson. I'm sure it's fine. Slim Gomez, the ranch's ramrod, is back, so give him a shout. I'll give Slim a head up that you're coming. The Beaumonts have several tractors for you to choose from, and since Reed asked you to plant a hay lot—"

"Reed saved my butt, Callie. He saved my farm."

"How did he do that?"

"Don't you know? He handed me a check for twenty grand for the hay lot, to catch up on my mortgage and for first dibs at my animals."

"You haven't sold Billy's animals, have you?"

"Not now I'm not, and I owe it all to Reed."

"Thank goodness. Billy would have been devastated."

"I know. But would you tell Slim that I'll be over for the tractor tomorrow? I want to get started plowing and planting."

"Will do, Mr. Waterson."

"Bill. Call me Bill."

"Okay, Bill."

Callie looked through her spreadsheets that she'd had with her, and didn't see a transaction totaling twenty thousand dollars. She would have remembered such an amount.

Reed must have used his stock earnings.

She remembered little Billy during the first-grade tour. He was so sad. She and Reed had talked about how to help the Watersons, and it seemed that Reed solved the problem.

The Beaumonts certainly had enough land for a hay lot, but Callie knew that Reed had done it for the Watersons.

Her heart warmed even more toward Reed. He'd used his play money.

Callie walked into the kitchen where her mother was washing some glasses.

"Mom, I'm going to get plane tickets to the next PBR event. It's this weekend in Colorado Springs. I have to talk to Reed."

"Are you going to tell him that you're coming?"

"I don't think so, Mom. Let me surprise him."

A WEEK AFTER NASHVILLE, Reed won the Colorado Springs PBR event. Jesse came in second, and Luke came in third.

"The Beaumont Big Guns have tied up the first three positions again, ladies and gentlemen. Let's give them a big round of applause."

The arena erupted into clapping and whistles. Reed stood in front of the now-empty chutes, accepting belt buckles, checks and saddles from the arena announcer.

"And, ladies and gentlemen, boys and girls, all the bull riders will be signing autographs in the arena right now."

The line started forming as the bull riders took their places at tables, mostly in alphabetical order.

"Hi. Who should I make this out to?"

"Callie Wainright."

Reed's head jerked up. "Callie? What? When? Were you here for the bull riding?"

"I sure was, Reed. Excellent riding."

"Thanks, Callie."

"I was nervous when you drew Jimbo. At least you rode him. And a ninety-two-point ride!"

"And when he tossed me off, I was able to outrun him."

"Congratulations, Reed."

He nodded. "Hey, how'd you get here, Callie?"

"Plane. I took the weekend off. I needed it."

"How about a late dinner with me?"

"I thought you'd never ask."

"Where are you staying?"

"The host hotel."

"Great. I'm there, too. Do you mind waiting for me while I finish the signing?"

She smiled. "I don't mind at all. I'm used to waiting for you."

Reed whistled and held up his hand, and a man with credential tags came running. "Jud, would you mind getting Callie a chair? She's going to sit by me and wait."

"Sure, Reed." Jud went running, and hustled back with a chair. "There you go, Miss Callie."

"Thanks, Jud."

He tweaked the brim of his hat to her, and Callie's heart warmed. Reed was a cowboy, a special breed.

She watched as Reed signed posters, ball caps, cowboy hats, T-shirts and the like. He still drew the line at signing body parts.

"Sorry, darlin'. I wouldn't want my daughter to go around asking a stranger to sign her stomach, and neither should you. How about an autographed picture instead?"

He had old-school values, Callie thought. She liked that about him. She liked a lot of things about him.

They walked hand-in-hand to the hotel. It was a wonderful night, just a little bit cool. Reed took his jacket off and wrapped it around her shoulders.

He took her hand and she wished they could walk like this together a bit longer, but they only had a block to go.

There was a big fan presence at the hotel and Reed took the time to greet everyone. Then he turned to Callie, "How about room service, if you don't mind? I'd like to concentrate on you, Callie. We have a lot to catch up on."

They went to her room because he was sharing his with Jesse this time. They ordered burgers and fries and milk shakes.

"Tell me, what brought you to Colorado Springs?"

"You did, Reed. I have a couple of things to discuss with you."

He sat on the desk chair and Callie sat on the bed. "Shoot."

"Tell me about twenty thousand dollars going to Bill Waterson. I don't have a record of it."

He was silent for a moment. "I know you don't have a record of it. I used my play money, not any that relates to the ranch."

"And by your play money, I assume you mean your—"

"Stock-trading money. Or as you would call it, my gambling money."

She nodded. "You paid for a hay lot that you don't really need, right?"

He shrugged his shoulders. "Yeah, but hopefully, Bill Waterson won't figure that out. Besides, the hay won't go to waste. I just negotiated a contract to supply it to the stock contractors at PBR events. This way, they won't have to transport their own. I'll transport it and give the profits to Bill. Bill will work hard, and eventually he'll make a profit. I'll see to that."

"Reed, I—"

"Like I said. It's not money I need. It's money I play with."

"What else do you do with your stock money?"

"If I hear of someone who needs it, and if it's a good cause, I see that they get it."

"Anonymously?" she asked, wide-eyed.

"Most of the time."

"That's nice of you, Reed. Really nice. And this all comes from your investment money?"

He shrugged. "Yeah."

"You're something else, Reed. Something else."

"Why all the questions, Callie?"

"I just wanted to know. I wanted to know if you're a gambler like my father, always chasing a dollar, then spending that last dollar on a lottery ticket."

"So what did you figure out?"

"No, Reed. I'm finally getting it. You're like Robin Hood or something, only you give your stock profits to those who need it. Your play money, as you call it."

"Communication, Callie. We have to be able to talk to one another, and listen." He sighed. "I guess I'll quit if it still bothers you."

"Don't you dare quit playing the stock market!" Callie couldn't believe that those words came out of her mouth. "You use your profits for good. Everyone told me that you weren't a gambler and that includes the worst one alive, my father."

"So everything's fine between us?" Reed asked.

"No. There's one thing still pending."

"What's that?" he asked.

"Remember how you said that you'd do an activity of my choice?"

"I do. Have you decided what you'd like to do?"

"I sure have."

"Movie? Bowling? What?"

"I want you to make love to me, Reed," she said, walking over to massage his shoulders. "That's what I want. I want you to make love to me."

As Reed stood up and grinned. Then there was a knock on the door.

"Room service."

"That's just my luck." Reed laughed. "Later?" He gave her a smoldering kiss, a promise of things to come.

It took a while for Callie to find her voice. "Later."

Chapter Fifteen

"I'm going to take a shower, Callie. Join me."

Reed began removing his clothes, and Callie could only stare at the sight. He was comfortable in his body. He unbuttoned his white shirt with all the logos and tossed it on the bed, undid the button on his jeans and pulled down his zipper.

Callie was so mesmerized that she barely blinked. There was something so carefree and easygoing about Reed that it pulled her to him. So did his hard chest and six-pack abs.

His jeans were gone and he was wearing just boxers. Soon, his underwear disappeared, along with his socks.

He stood there in his naked glory without a care in the world. "If you're going to join me, you'd better catch up. I'm naked here."

"And you look fabulous, Reed, She lightly ran her fingers over the scars on his back and chest. They were scars from bull riding. Strangely, they didn't mar his manliness; they only added to it.

Fully clothed, Callie stood behind Reed, reaching around his body, running her hands over his chest, his nipples, feeling his hard abs, and lower, lower still until she felt his erection.

"Whoa, Callie. I don't want it to be over before we start." He took some deep breaths and turned toward her.

"Undress for me while I put this thing on." A condom appeared in his hand. He took it out of the small, square wrapper and rolled it onto his hard length.

Watching Reed put the condom on, set Callie's heart to racing. If Reed wanted a sexy striptease, it wasn't going to happen. Callie wanted him now!

She hurriedly got out of her clothes and, with an eager, "Yee-haw," she pinned Reed on the bed.

He laughed as Callie kissed him along his stubble. She lingered at his nipples and down his muscled chest.

Reversing their positions, it was Reed's turn to have her under him. "I want to make this good for you, Callie. After all, it's the activity that you asked for. Right?"

"Right! Now quit talking and let's have some action!" She was breathless just thinking of what was to come.

Reed laughed. "I guess this isn't going to be slow, huh?"

"Reed…please! I want you."

She spread her legs and he looked down at her closed eyes. "Open your eyes for me, Callie. I want you to know that it's me making love to you."

"I know that, Reed."

With a strong thrust, he entered her and waited until she started to move in an erotic rhythm. He kissed her neck and took a nipple into his mouth, biting it softly.

"Oh, my, Reed. Oh…"

He moved to the other nipple and he received the same reaction. He waited for Callie to catch up with him, and when she reached her climax, he let himself go.

They clung to one another, then spooned together, trying to catch their breaths.

"Let's do it again!" Callie said with a burst of energy.

"This time I'm not going for the gold buckle, I'm going to take it slow and easy."

Callie put her hand in his. "Challenge accepted."

"Callie, loving you will never be a challenge. I've always been yours."

"And although I've dated some major losers over the past several years, I think I drove them away. They just weren't you, Reed. None of them could compare."

They made love again, this time leisurely and unhurried, and as she drifted off to sleep, Callie knew she was so happy that she was going to burst.

THE NEXT DAY was another bull-riding event. Reed was on fire and, after making love with Callie last night, he was walking on sunshine with his cowboy boots. Finally, Reed thought, everything had been resolved between them and he could show her how much he loved her.

They certainly were compatible in bed, and she finally understood that he wasn't a gambler. When the time was right, he was going to ask Callie to marry him.

He got Callie a seat in the section reserved for the wives and girlfriends of the bull riders. It was close to the chutes, and Reed couldn't take his eyes off her.

But he needed to concentrate on his job at hand.

He had an engagement ring for her. The same ring that he'd been carrying with him in its little velvet box in a corner of his gear bag for ten years.

Over the years, the gear bags came and went, but he'd made sure that he had the ring. He always thought of it as a symbol of hope that someday he and Callie would be together again.

And now they were.

But he didn't want to ask her to marry him in Colorado Springs, or Billings, Montana, or even Las Vegas.

He wanted to ask Callie to marry him on the bank of the Beaumont River where they'd first made love. In fact, if he could arrange it, he'd have an extra surprise for her.

Reed would fly home with her after the event was over, and he'd ask Callie to marry him.

It was about time!

REED DREW WHITE WHALE in the final round. The bull was known for his spinning abilities and meanness when the ride was over. Reed was warned by the bullfighters to hustle away from White Whale and climb the fence surrounding the arena if necessary.

But if Reed could last eight seconds on White Whale, he could get a ninety-point ride.

It was cowboy up for him.

He loaded his bull rope with rosin and worked it until the stuff was as sticky as possible. Then he wrapped his hand.

Just before he nodded his head, he quickly looked at Callie. She had her hands clenched in her lap. She didn't have to worry about him. He knew exactly what White Whale was going to do.

He slipped on his teeth guard. Then he nodded his head. "Buck 'em, boys."

White Whale exploded out of the chute gate. The massive bull leaped into the air on all fours, and Reed stayed with him. Then White Whale played all his tricks to get Reed off—a belly roll, a fake to the left. Then a fake to the right. Then the bull spun so fast, it made Reed's head feel like it was going to explode. But still, he stayed with him.

Reed heard the buzzer above the roar of the crowd.

Eight seconds. He'd ridden White Whale!

Reed didn't know that he was the bounty bull until he heard the announcer say so.

Twelve thousand dollars was in the pot. He knew just what to do with the extra money. Reed knew of a fellow bull rider who'd just bought a ranch, and the house needed work before he could move in his young family. The extra money would help them out.

Reed made a ninety-four-point ride and the confetti cannons blew their colorful paper. Reed was now in the lead with seven more riders left to go.

They didn't come close to Reed's score. No one else could beat him, and Reed was declared the winner.

He asked Jud, the coordinator, to bring Callie to the winner's circle, and Jud obliged. Callie stood next to him, smiling.

"Congratulations, Reed. I'm happy for you."

Reed gathered her into his arms and gave her a big kiss. The audience roared in approval.

Reed was presented with yet another belt buckle, another saddle and a rifle.

He turned to Callie and gave her the buckle. "Colorado Springs will always have a special place in my heart. I'd like for you to remember it, too."

Callie whispered. "I'll never forget it."

"It's a great day for a picnic," Callie said, handing Reed a roast beef sandwich. "We couldn't ask for better weather. And I just love this spot. It's the best spot on your ranch, don't you think?"

"I sure do. It's our spot, Callie. And you know, I come up here to think all the time."

"What do you think about, Reed?"

"Mostly you, darlin'."

Her eyes opened wide. "Me?"

"Yeah. Mostly you. All the time. You."

"I think of you a lot, too. All the time, Reed Beaumont."

He put his sandwich down on the paper plate and covered it with a napkin. He held out his hand to Callie and she took it. "Come with me. I want to take a walk along the river."

"You don't want to eat?"

"Later."

"Should I put my shoes on?" she asked.

"Hell, no. Let's go wading in the water."

The water was cold until they got used to it. Reed led Callie to a rock and she sat with her feet in the water.

"If I owned this land, I'd have my feet in the water every day."

"If you owned this land, what would you do with your house on Elm?"

"I'd let my mother have it," she declared.

"And speaking of money, I want you to know that I'll be giving the twelve grand that I received for the bounty bull to a fellow rider who needs it for his family."

"That's so sweet of you, Reed."

"Callie, what if we were married and it was *our* money?"

"But we're not married and it's not our money."

"Let's just pretend it's our money."

"If it were ours and it was an extra windfall? I'd do the same thing."

"That's wonderful!"

"Reed, why all the questions?"

"I'm glad to know that we feel the same about money."

"That it's like manure and should be spread around?"

He gave her a big kiss. "Exactly."

She grinned. "You like playing Robin Hood, don't you?"

"More than anything." He chuckled, then turned serious. "Callie, I'm going to probably ride until the PBR ends in Vegas in November. Will you travel with me?"

"Yes. As long as I could come back during the week and handle my business," she said. "I sure will get frequent-flier miles."

"And you can use some of mine."

He took her hand and led her out of the water.

He brought her to stand on some grassland, where he dropped to one knee and took her hand.

"Callie Wainright, will you marry me and make me a very happy cowboy?"

"I thought you'd never ask!"

He pulled out the battered black velvet case. "This ring has been kicking around in my gear bag forever." He opened the box.

Callie's heart soared. "It's beautiful, Reed. Thank you!" She pulled him to his feet and they kissed.

"And, Callie? The land that we're standing on is ours. I picked out ten acres by our special section of the creek to build a house on. My other two brothers each have ten acres, too. You just tell the architect the kind of house you'd like and it's yours."

"Reed, things are just going so fast!"

"I know! Isn't it great? But do you like the ring?"

"Of course, I do, Reed. For heaven's sake, you could have given me a cigar band and I'd be thrilled."

"Um, uh...would you like to wear it?"

"Of course!"

He slipped the ring on her finger. "Perfect."

"Yes, it is, Reed."

"Are you going to say it?"

"What?" she asked.

"Say that you'll marry me."

"I thought I did."

He shook his head. "Not really."

"Of course, I'll marry you! I love you, you crazy cow-boy."

"Finally," they said together as Reed tossed his hat into the air.

"Yee-haw!"

Epilogue

A few months later

THE BEAUMONT BULLETIN
Around Our Town
Suzy Finkleman, Editor

Callie Wainright and Reed Beaumont were married under the historic wrought iron arch leading to the equally historic Beaumont Ranch yesterday.

Most of Beaumont turned out for a night of eating, drinking and dancing at Poppa Al's Restaurant. The Cowhand Band kept everyone boot scootin' until the wee hours of the morning.

The bride looked stunning in a simple gown that her mother had made of white satin with a print of tiny daisies. Peeking out from under her gown were green and pink cowboy boots. She carried a bouquet of white roses and daisies.

The groom looked dashing in traditional Western attire: a black coat and black pants, a crisp, white shirt, bolo tie and a belt buckle the size of Texas. He wore black snakeskin boots and a black Resistol hat.

The matron of honor was Amber Chapman Beaumont, wife of Luke Beaumont. Bridesmaids were Sarah Lock, Donna Palmeri, Margie Goldstein and Patti Gaddo.

Standing up for the groom were the bride's twin brothers, Joe and John Wainright, and the groom's brothers, Luke and Jesse Beaumont.

Guests dined on a buffet of steak, chicken, barbecue, pasta and various salads.

The new Mr. and Mrs. Beaumont requested that in lieu of gifts, donations be made to a charity of the guest's choice.

The couple left for their honeymoon in Las Vegas, where the groom will be riding for the Professional Bull Riders World Championship in a five-day event.

When asked about the championship, the groom stated, "After the Finals in Vegas, I'm going to retire. I have some other things I'd like to do around the ranch."

A little bird told me that he's going to open his own bull-riding school with older brother, Luke Beaumont. The youngest of the clan, Jesse, is still going to be riding with the PBR.

The bride stated that she would like to write a book about the history of the Beaumont Ranch, starting with the 1889 Oklahoma Land Rush. She further stated that the book and her business, Personable Assistance, will keep her busy.

And they both want to pursue advanced degrees at OSU.

I know of two other little items that will be keeping both the bride and groom busy. After all, twins are common in the bride's family!

See you around our beautiful town.

Suzy

* * * * *

If you enjoyed this novel, don't miss
THE COWBOY AND THE COP,
the previous book in Christine Wenger's
GOLD BUCKLE COWBOYS *miniseries,*
available now from Harlequin Western Romance!

We hope you enjoyed this story from
Harlequin® Western Romance.

Harlequin® Western Romance is coming to an
end, but community, cowboys and true love are
here to stay. Starting July 2018, discover more
heartfelt tales of family and friendship from
Harlequin® Special Edition.

Romance is for life, and these stories show that
every chapter in a relationship has its challenges
and delights and that love can be
renewed with each turn of the page!

Look for six *new* romances every month
from **Harlequin® Special Edition!**
Available wherever books are sold.

Get 2 Free Books,
Plus 2 Free Gifts—
just for trying the Reader Service!

HARLEQUIN
SPECIAL EDITION

YES! Please send me 2 FREE Harlequin® Special Edition novels and my 2 FREE gifts (gifts are worth about $10 retail). After receiving them, if I don't wish to receive any more books, I can return the shipping statement marked "cancel." If I don't cancel, I will receive 6 brand-new novels every month and be billed just $4.99 per book in the U.S. or $5.74 per book in Canada. That's a savings of at least 12% off the cover price! It's quite a bargain! Shipping and handling is just 50¢ per book in the U.S. and 75¢ per book in Canada*. I understand that accepting the 2 free books and gifts places me under no obligation to buy anything. I can always return a shipment and cancel at any time. The free books and gifts are mine to keep no matter what I decide.

235/335 HDN GMWS

Name _____ (PLEASE PRINT)

Address _____ Apt. #

City _____ State/Province _____ Zip/Postal Code

Signature (if under 18, a parent or guardian must sign)

Mail to the **Reader Service:**
IN U.S.A.: P.O. Box 1341, Buffalo, NY 14240-8531
IN CANADA: P.O. Box 603, Fort Erie, Ontario L2A 5X3

Want to try two free books from another line?
Call 1-800-873-8635 or visit www.ReaderService.com.

*Terms and prices subject to change without notice. Prices do not include applicable taxes. Sales tax applicable in N.Y. Canadian residents will be charged applicable taxes. Offer not valid in Quebec. This offer is limited to one order per household. Books received may not be as shown. Not valid for current subscribers to Harlequin® Special Edition books. All orders subject to approval. Credit or debit balances in a customer's account(s) may be offset by any other outstanding balance owed by or to the customer. Please allow 4 to 6 weeks for delivery. Offer available while quantities last.

Your Privacy—The Reader Service is committed to protecting your privacy. Our Privacy Policy is available online at www.ReaderService.com or upon request from the Reader Service.

We make a portion of our mailing list available to reputable third parties that offer products we believe may interest you. If you prefer that we not exchange your name with third parties, or if you wish to clarify or modify your communication preferences, please visit us at www.ReaderService.com/consumerschoice or write to us at Reader Service Preference Service, P.O. Box 9062, Buffalo, NY 14240-9062. Include your complete name and address.

HSE17R3

SPECIAL EXCERPT FROM

⒣ HARLEQUIN®

Western Romance

Ryder Mitchell is shocked to see Becca Hartman back in Montana. The beautiful single mom is keeping secrets about his estranged sister, but he's determined to learn the truth.

Read on for a sneak preview of
TO TRUST A RANCHER by Debbi Rawlins,
*the latest book in the **MADE IN MONTANA** series,*
available May 2018 wherever Harlequin®
Western Romance books and ebooks are sold.

Eyes widening, she gasped. "Ryder."

"Hello, Becca."

"Hi." Her gaze darted briefly to the small boy next to her. "This is a surprise."

"That's an understatement." Ryder did a quick mental calculation. The boy would've been two years old when Becca's grandmother died. As far as he knew, Shirley hadn't mentioned anything about Becca having a kid. And when it came to what little news they got about Amy and Becca in LA, his mom never skipped a word.

"Right." She cleared her throat. "I planned on calling you and your mom later."

He raised his eyebrows.

"You know, after we settled in. We just got to town an hour ago."

Okay, maybe she was telling the truth. But why look so nervous? "I hope by *we* you mean Amy," he said, holding Becca's gaze. "Is she here?"

She shook her head. Sadness flickered in her hazel eyes before she blinked and looked away. "I think she had other plans for the—" She pressed her lips together and swallowed.

"What? For Thanksgiving? Let's see, that makes seven of them that she's missed now?"

"I'm not her keeper," Becca said, her voice barely a whisper. "Your sister does what she wants."

"Aunt Amy gave me a neato truck." The kid grinned up at him. "You wanna see it?"

Ryder felt a surge of relief. He didn't know what had given him the sick feeling that something bad had happened to Amy. If that were true, she wouldn't be buying the kid toys. "Hey, sport."

"Sport?" The boy wrinkled his nose. "My name is Noah."

"Sorry, Noah. I'm Ryder." He stuck his hand out. The kid slapped his palm against Ryder's and started giggling.

In spite of himself, Ryder smiled. Whatever was up with Amy wasn't Becca's son's fault. Ryder was seven years older than his sister and hadn't paid much attention to her friends, but he remembered Becca

When he looked back up at her, he saw the tears in her eyes before she blinked them away.

The relief he'd felt moments ago disappeared. Something was wrong, and Becca knew the truth.

Don't miss TO TRUST A RANCHER by Debbi Rawlins, available May 2018 wherever Harlequin® Western Romance books and ebooks are sold.

www.Harlequin.com

HWREXP0418

Looking for more satisfying love stories
with community and family at their core?

Check out **Harlequin®** Special Edition
and **Harlequin®** Western Romance books!

New books available every month!

CONNECT WITH US AT:

Harlequin.com/Community

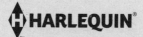

**ROMANCE WHEN
YOU NEED IT**

HFGENRE2017R

Reward the book lover in you!

Earn points from all your Harlequin book purchases from wherever you shop.

Turn your points into *FREE BOOKS* of your choice
OR
EXCLUSIVE GIFTS from your favorite authors or series.

Join for FREE today at
www.HarlequinMyRewards.com.

Harlequin My Rewards is a free program (no fees) without any commitments or obligations.

MYR17